Júlio Ribeiro

FLESH

Translated and introduced by
William Barne

MODERN HUMANITIES RESEARCH ASSOCIATION
2011

Published by

The Modern Humanities Research Association,
1 Carlton House Terrace
London SW1Y 5AF

© The Modern Humanities Research Association, 2011

William Barne has asserted his right under the Copyright, Designs and Patents Act 1988 to be identified as the author of this work.

Parts of this work may be reproduced as permitted under legal provisions for fair dealing (or fair use) for the purposes of research, private study, criticism, or review, or when a relevant collective licensing agreement is in place. All other reproduction requires the written permission of the copyright holder who may be contacted at rights@mhra.org.uk.

First published 2011

ISBN 978-1-907322-28-0

Copies may be ordered from www.translations.mhra.org.uk

CONTENTS

Acknowledgements   vii

Introduction   ix

Flesh

  Chapter 1   5

  Chapter 2   9

  Chapter 3   13

  Chapter 4   17

  Chapter 5   21

  Chapter 6   27

  Chapter 7   33

  Chapter 8   40

  Chapter 9   47

  Chapter 10   56

  Chapter 11   63

  Chapter 12   80

  Chapter 13   93

  Chapter 14   108

  Chapter 15   117

  Chapter 16   121

  Chapter 17   127

  Chapter 18   135

ACKNOWLEDGEMENTS

This translation is dedicated to my wife Magdalena who introduced me to Brazil and its literature, and supported me in this project.

A number of Brazilian friends assisted me with the comprehension of the text, in particular the writer Antonella Sigaud.

I am especially grateful to Ariano Farias, who read the whole text and translation in parallel, elucidating difficult passages in the original and suggesting solutions for the translation.

INTRODUCTION

'The presence of Júlio Ribeiro in the history of the Brazilian novel is a mistake. Júlio Ribeiro is an author outside literature.'

(Álvaro Lins, 1952).

Júlio Ribeiro and Naturalism in Brazil

Júlio Ribeiro (1845–1890) was a Brazilian journalist, grammarian and writer. Republican, abolitionist and free-thinker, widely read and highly educated (largely self-taught), his two novels bracket a writing career which was devoted principally to journalism, but also included philological works and vehement political pamphleteering. He lived to see slavery abolished and the Republic founded before he died of tuberculosis at the age of only 45. On the foundation of the Brazilian Academy of Letters in 1896 he was selected as the patron of chair N° 24 by its founder, Garcia Redondo.

After a childhood education with his schoolmistress mother he entered military school in Rio de Janeiro in 1862; however, after three years he abandoned an army career and devoted himself to teaching, before turning to writing in various forms. He founded at least three journals — *O Sorocabano* (1870–72), *A Procelária* and the republican organ *O Debate* — and collaborated in several more. As a modernizing linguist he wrote *General outlines of linguistics* (1880), *Portuguese Grammar* (1881) and a *New grammar of the Latin language* (published posthumously in 1896). He also translated Edgar Allan Poe's *The Murders in the Rue Morgue*.

His first essay in fiction was *Padre Belchior de Pontes* (1876/7), a two-volume romance based on a historical figure in which the author, then a Presbyterian, attacked the Jesuits. The book was well received but remains a minor work. At some time he fell under the influence of the French novelist Émile Zola, and his second novel and lasting contribution to Brazilian literature, *Flesh* (*A Carne*), published in May 1888, is prefaced by a dedication to Zola which ends with a quotation from Dante: 'Tu duca, tu signore, tu maestro'. It was this novel which so provoked the ire of the critic Álvaro Lins more than sixty years after its publication.

A Naturalist movement was already established in Brazil, with at least five other authors who published novels in the style of Zola. Inglês de Sousa published *O Cacaulista* and *História de um Pescador*, with a focus on Amazon indians, as early as 1876, but only became widely known with *O Missionário* in 1891. The best-known of the group was Aluísio Azevedo, who effectively inaugurated Naturalism in Brazil with *O Mulato* (1881), a shocking revelation of the racial question. He planned a series of five Brazilian novels imitating Zola's *Rougon-Macquart* series, of which only *Casa de pensão* (1884) and *O Cortiço* (1890) were published.

Flesh appeared months before the final abolition of slavery and only 18 months before the abolition of the monarchy, both triumphs for which Ribeiro had campaigned. In conformance with Naturalist principles and Ribeiro's convictions, *Flesh* addresses a number of social issues: slavery and its associated brutality, the backwardness of rural areas under conservative landowners, the impunity of the elite, racial and social prejudice etc., as well as suicide. However, the principal social theme of the book is the position of women in society — and associated with this, the theme of sexuality and sexual liberation, as well as divorce and a scathing attack on the institution of marriage.

The novel tells the story of Lenita, an exceptional young woman in contemporary Brazil, rich, intelligent and independent, who embarks on an illicit affair with a married but separated man, as a result of which she becomes pregnant. Obliged by social mores to find a legal father for the child, divorce not yet being recognized in Brazil, she abandons the *fazenda* (country estate) and her lover to marry a conventional lawyer who has recently proposed to her.

The structure is simple and monolinear — indeed the work is structurally more of a long short story or *novella*, very different from the multiple narrative threads generally found in Zola's novels. The style is very clear and forceful with no punches pulled, for example in the brutal scene where the old negro 'sorcerer' is burnt alive, or the whipping of the runaway slave.

The Naturalist aesthetic is apparent in descriptions of the city, countryside and the jungle, including the sugar harvest, a description of the port of Santos, and especially the train connecting the port with São Paulo. This is an excuse for Ribeiro to express his fascination with, and belief in, technological development. He doubtless walked down the track as Manuel Barbosa does in the novel, and we may suppose that this is not the only autobiographical aspect of the characterisation of Barbosa. The stylistic weakness of the aesthetic as a supposed portrayal of reality is apparent too in

Lenita's education, which is all-embracing to a frankly improbable degree, as contemporary critics were quick to point out.

The concentration of Ribeiro's writing is remarkable, perhaps comparable to that of Maupassant. The first chapter, a little over three pages long, is sufficient to cover Lenita's early life and see her installed in the *fazenda*, and yet the reader does not feel that the author has skimped the story. The principal characteristics of the heroine are already clearly established — her superior mentality, her independence and her reaction to the death of her father. As with Maupassant we feel that we have read much more than is actually written.

A celebrated controversy

Perhaps the most revolutionary aspect of the book in terms of social organization is its portrayal of Lenita as an educated and independent woman in a society which expected its females to be no more than decorative adjuncts to their husbands. Lenita is a woman of 'immense superiority'. We see her in society putting pretentious pedants to flight, and later her intellect is portrayed as equal to that of Barbosa, who succinctly describes what she should have been by conventional standards:

> I knew that she was very well-educated, but I thought that meant well-educated in the way of girls in general, especially in Brazil — piano, singing, four fingers of French, two of English, two of geography and… that's that! But I was mistaken; Miss Helena is astonishingly erudite, indeed, she has the true scientific spirit. She possesses a superior mind, admirably cultivated.

Lenita and Barbosa — himself an above average intellect — are portrayed as equals, discussing many topics of scientific interest and undertaking experiments together. Moreover she rides (no doubt astride!) and shoots and has a cool head — and a strong will, as we see, for example, when she decides to abandon the *fazenda*, against the wishes of the Colonel and his wife: 'The supplications of the invalid, the Colonel's pouting insistence, were fruitless.'

Furthermore, it is she who finally crystallises the relationship with Barbosa, firstly by declaring her love for him — she makes 'the confession which no woman ever wants to be the first to make' when she thinks she is dying — and then by going to his room at night.

And here we come to the point that generated the immense controversy which surrounded the novel from its first appearance, leading it to be dubbed by contemporaries 'one of the most discussed and popular books in the country'; for all the other debatable aspects of the work were subsumed in the scandal aroused by its presentation of female sexuality. The theme of Lenita's sexual awakening is carefully structured through the novel, from her hallucination in Chapter 3, through the descriptions of the swarming fertility of the jungle (reminiscent of Zola's *La Faute de l'abbé Mouret*) and the mating of the cattle, up to the scenes of her passion with Barbosa. Although they are written for the most part in a deliberately scientific (Naturalist) tone, and although the description of the critical moment when Lenita loses her virginity is practically poetic, some of these passages are still startling today, and were far outside the pale of the conventional in the late nineteenth century.

Of course, Ribeiro was writing to provoke, starting with the whiff of pornography contained in the title. Reaction from the conservative flank was immediate and fierce. Alfredo Pujol (1865–1930), then a law student and later a writer and politician, a young republican who might be expected to be sympathetic to Ribeiro's artistic and political aims, was one of the first to launch a violent attack on the book, in an article published in the *Diário Mercantil* on 12 August 1888: 'Júlio Ribeiro's "Flesh"'.

But this was no more than a prelude to the attack of the principal critic, a Portuguese priest, Padre José Joaquim Senna Freitas, who wrote articles in the *Diário Mercantil* from 26 September of the same year under the punning title 'A Carniça' (Carrion) as a '…warning to the public stomach against this illicit sale of putrid flesh, on offer at 3$000 a slice in the literary butcher's shops of São Paulo'. Senna Freitas posed as the defender of Brazilian morals and appealed to Ribeiro to think that honest women, like the writer's own wife and young daughters (with whom the priest was acquainted) would be the readers of a book describing how a young woman like themselves could 'fall at one bound from honesty to prostitution'. His words closely foreshadow the famous obscenity trial over *Lady Chatterley's Lover* (Italy, 1928), a similar literary *cause célèbre*, after it was finally published in England in 1960. Ribeiro, a strong anti-clericalist, responded (and turned the pun on the priest) in a series of articles 'O Urubú Senna Freitas' (Senna Freitas, the Vulture) as a reaction to the criticisms of '…the liturgical buffoon, the clown in a cassock', declaring: 'I will not reply to his criticisms, I will simply cut him down to size' — as he went on to do, pointing out grammatical and other errors in the priest's writing rather than defending his own novel. The articles of the two writers were later compiled and published together by Orígenes Lessa, a descendant of Ribeiro, under the title *Uma Polêmica Célebre* (*A Celebrated Controversy*) in 1934, at which date the novel was still considered 'daring'.

José Veríssimo (1857-1916), co-founder of the Brazilian Academy of Letters, described the book in an essay, 'The Naturalist Romance in Brazil' (1889), as 'the monstrous childbirth of an artistically sick brain'. His objections were principally on the grounds of classical good taste and the improbability of the narrative. His venom had softened somewhat by 1915, when he admits that the 'vigour' of some of the descriptions saves the novel from absolute failure and points to affiliation to the 'tightest moulds of Zolism' and the 'scandalously obscene features of the romance' as the roots of his objections (*History of Brazilian Literature*, 1916).

Ribeiro must have had his supporters also, as his selection as patron of a chair in the Brazilian Academy of Letters indicates, but they appear to have left him to defend himself.

Not surprisingly with such publicity, the novel sold well from its first appearance. In parallel with continued establishment disapproval, the young and liberal read it keenly, and no doubt many of those who criticized it in public drew hypocritical pleasure from scanning its pages in private. At least four film versions were made. The fate of the first by Carmen Santos (1924) is not recorded, but it cannot have had much impact since a second version was filmed only the following year: Túlio and Ricci (1925) struggled to cope with presenting the sexual episodes, using an allegory of mating cattle (based on the text) to represent Barbosa's and Lenita's consummation of their love. The actress who played Lenita was kept in the dark as to the real meaning of some scenes as it was feared that she might walk off the set. The next attempt by Waldyr Cruz (1952) failed at the box office, reportedly due to prejudice against its 'immorality'. The 1975 version by José Marreco in the context of the popular comedy genre of *pornochanchada* cinema hardly raised an eyebrow, and even won an award for its photography.

Meanwhile, disapproval in some literary circles continued for decades. Lúcia Miguel Pereira, in *Prose Fiction 1870-1920* (*History of Brazilian Literature Vol. XII*, under the direction of Álvaro Lins, 1950), can still write:

> The case of Júlio Ribeiro is typical. A philologist and valiant polemicist [...], he allowed himself to be entrapped by the famous studies of temperament. Despite his descriptive powers, he managed only to compose a ridiculous book. The superior woman whom he wanted to show, struggling at the same time with the demands of the flesh and social conventions, resulted in an unbearable pedant and a vulgar story. The author did not draw her from life but from books.

In 1952, the same Álvaro Lins simply banished Ribeiro from Brazil's literature: 'I believe ... that he does not deserve to be considered or studied in any publication of a strictly literary character' (*Two Naturalists: Aluísio Azevedo and Júlio Ribeiro*).

Public support for Ribeiro came from the distinguished Brazilian poet Manuel Bandeira (1886–1968), in his inaugural speech in the Brazilian Academy of Letters (1940), who claimed that *Flesh* '... deserved to remain, like so many other romantic and Realist novels, in the literary history of Brazil.' He repeated the message when in 1945 the Academy arranged an act of homage to mark the centenary of Ribeiro's birth, evidence that the poet who sat in chair N° 24 was not alone in valuing the author of *Flesh*.

The loosening of strict conventional standards in the following decades brought relief to *Flesh* in Brazil, as it did to *Lady Chatterley's Lover* in England, where the publishers who had finally dared to print it were acquitted. Today *Flesh* is a recognized and respected part of Brazil's literary canon. Massaud Moisés in his *History of Brazilian Literature: Realism and Symbolism* (2001) summarises the criticisms levelled at the book and then goes on:

> All this may be true, incontestable even, but no unbiased reader will deny the qualities of the work, starting with the fragrance of the depiction of a São Paulo *fazenda* around 1887, including the scenes linked to slavery, and ending with the concise, idiomatic, rounded phrasing, and, last but not least, the plasticity of the erotic scenes. Qualities of a great writer, who wasted his talents for fiction by sticking too closely to the formula learnt from Zola; far above the average of his time and incomparable if we view him against the gallery of the following generation. [...] More powerful than the eroticism ... is the denunciation of the ethical standards of the bourgeoisie triumphant. And in this

the novel rises to the level of the best that Brazilian Naturalism produced, not excluding the works of Aluísio Azevedo.

On the translation

In rendering the speech of the slaves Ribeiro at times uses a phonetic representation which today might not be considered 'politically correct'. In order to be faithful both to the original text and to the principles of Naturalism, in my translation I have attempted, where the original is represented in this way, to indicate a non-specific Caribbean accent. This is in no way intended to be demeaning to the people of those islands, of whom I have warm memories, having lived there for five years. I have also borrowed Caribbean common plant names.

Footnotes

I have tried to elucidate references which would have been recognizable to an educated Brazilian of the period, so long as the note adds something to what the reader may deduce and without entering into abstruse detail.

Selected references

Magalhães Bulhões, Marcelo. *Leituras do desejo; o erotismo no romance naturalista brasileira* (São Paulo: EdUSP, 2003).

Moisés, Massaud. *História da literatura brasileira: Realismo e simbolismo* (São Paulo: Cultrix, 2001).

Perdigão Lessa, David. 'A carne está na mesa: esquartejada, temperada e bem servida: Julio Ribeiro e a crítica literária', *Glaúks*, 7 (2007), 157–75.

<http://www.portalsaofrancisco.com.br/alfa/julio-ribeiro/julio-ribeiro.php> [contains a selection of articles of interest].

Ramos, Fernão; Miranda, Luiz Felipe. *Enciclopédia do cinema brasileiro* (São Paulo: Senac, 2000).

< http://www.avilainglesa.com/acarne.html> [refers to the 1952 film].

FLESH

To the Prince of Naturalism

Émile Zola

To my friends

Luis de Mattos

M.H. de Bittencourt

J.V. de Almeida and

Joaquim Elias;

To the distinguished physiologist

Dr. Miranda Azevedo

O.D.C.[1]

Júlio Ribeiro

---

[1] Offerit, dictat, consecrat.

To: M. Émile Zola[2]

I am not rash, I have no intention of trying to follow in your footsteps; it is not following in your footsteps to write a poor study with a hint of naturalism. You are not to be imitated but admired.

'We are heated' writes Ovid 'when the God who dwells in us is agitated.'[3] Well, the tiny God who dwells in me was agitated and I wrote *Flesh*.

It is not *L'Assommoir*, it is not *La Curée*, it is not *La Terre*; but *diantre*! a candle is not the sun, yet it casts light.

Here is my work, for what it is worth.

Will you accept my dedication of it to you? Why not! Kings, swollen with riches, do not disdain the puny gifts of poor peasants.

Allow me to offer you my unconditional homage, my liege, as a loyal servant, in the words of the Florentine poet:

Tu duca, tu signore, tu maestro.

São Paulo, 25 January, 1888.

Jules Ribeiro

---

[2] The original dedication is written in French.
[3] 'Est Deus in nobis, agitante calescimus illo.'

Chapter 1

Doctor Lopes Matoso was not exactly what you might call a fortunate man. At the age of eighteen, when he had barely finished his schooling, he lost his mother and father within a few months of one another.

His guardian was a friend of the family, a Colonel Barbosa, who made him continue with his studies and qualify in law.

The day after his graduation, his honest guardian entrusted him with the management of the large fortune which was his, saying: 'My boy, you are rich and qualified, and have a bright future before you. Now you should marry, have children and earn yourself a position. If I had a daughter, you would already have a bride; as I have not, you must seek one for yourself.'

Lopes Matoso wasted little time in looking and shortly afterwards married a cousin of whom he had always been fond, and with whom he lived blissfully for the space of two years.

At the beginning of the third year his wife died in childbirth, leaving him a baby girl.

Lopes Matoso reeled under the blow, but being a strong man he did not allow it to floor him completely. He picked himself up and accepted the new order of things imposed upon him by the brutal impartiality of nature.

He left his affairs in safe hands, moved to a smallholding which he owned not far from the city, left off seeing his friends and divided his time between scanning the pages of good books and caring for his daughter.

Thanks to her excellent nurse, she grew up strong and healthy, and at once became the life, the note of cheerfulness in the hermit's existence which Lopes Matoso had created for himself.

Friends seldom visited him, for he himself did not encourage them; he had no contact with members of his family.

Reading and writing, grammar, arithmetic, algebra, geometry, geography, history, French, Spanish, swimming, riding, gymnastics and music; in all of these Lopes Matoso instructed his daughter, for he was an expert in all of them. With her he read the Portuguese classics, the most important foreign authors, and the most interesting works of contemporary literature.

At the age of fourteen, Helena, or Lenita as she was called, was a strong, well-developed girl, with a fully formed character and an above average education.

Lopes Matoso saw that the time had come for another change in his life and moved back to the city.

There Lenita had the best tutors in languages and the sciences; she studied Italian, German, English, Latin and Greek. She did complete courses in mathematics and the physical sciences, and also became acquainted with the most complex social sciences. She found everything easy; it seemed that no field was closed to her extensive talents.

She began to appear and be noticed in society.

There was nothing pretentious or blue-stocking about her. Modest, withdrawn even, at the balls and parties which she not infrequently attended she was nevertheless able to surround herself with an aura of approachability, concealing with infinite art her immense superiority.

But it was a joy to see her when some freshly titled graduate, some tourist newly arrived from Paris or New York, tried to show off his learning or play the oracle in her presence. With charmingly simulated candour and a smile of condescending goodness she would enmesh the pedant in a web of treacherous questions, enclosing him little by little in a tightening ring of steel, until finally, with the most natural air in the world, she obliged him to contradict himself or reduced him to shamed silence.

Offers of marriage came thick and fast — Lopes Matoso consulted with his daughter.

'Keep turning them down, Father,' she replied. 'You don't need to ask me. You know that I have no desire to marry.'

'But Lenita, sooner or later you will have to.'

'One day, perhaps, but not now.'

'You know, I am beginning to think that I made a serious error in your education. I gave you knowledge far above the common run and the result is that I see you isolated on the heights to which I raised you. Man was made for woman and woman for man. Marriage is a necessity — I do not mean socially, I mean physiologically. Do you really not see any man worthy of you?'

'That is not the reason; I simply do not feel the need to marry. If I did, I would do so.'

'Even with a mediocre man?'

'Preferably with a mediocre man. Great men do not generally make good husbands. Besides, if great men almost invariably marry beneath themselves, why should not I, who in my Papa's eyes am a superior woman, do the same and choose a husband who is my inferior?'

'Yes, and have fools for children…'

'The children would take after me. Genetic theory tells us that the direct inheritance of genius and talent is most commonly from mother to son.'

'And not from father to daughter?'

'Of course; that is why I am what I am.'

'Flatterer!'

'The flatterer is a father who wants to make his daughter a prodigy at all costs, and has gone so far that even I am beginning to believe it. To return to the point, we have discussed the subject of marriage; let us not speak of it again.'

And they did not. Lopes Matoso continued to turn away her suitors with great expressions of regret — that his daughter did not wish to marry, that she was an original, that all his good advice was in vain, and a thousand words to soften the refusal.

And so Lenita's life continued until she was twenty-two, when one morning Lopes Matoso awoke complaining of an indescribable pain, a violent constriction of the chest. He burst into a fit of coughing and died on the spot, without the time so much as to call a doctor. He had succumbed to a pulmonary congestion.

Lenita became nearly distracted in her grief. The unexpectedness of the occurrence, the sudden, terrible void in her world, the superiority and cultivation of her spirit which shunned banal consolation, all contributed to aggravate her suffering.

The unhappy girl spent day after day in her room, refusing to receive visitors, eating some light sustenance almost unconsciously at the insistence of her maids.

Finally she reacted against her grief. Pale, her pallor emphasised by her mourning garments, she appeared before her father's friends to receive their tiresome, formal condolences, and tried somehow or other to adapt herself to the solitary life which opened up before her, a desolate life bare of affection and peopled with painful memories. She set about making suitable arrangements for the management of her affairs and wrote to Colonel Barbosa proposing to retire temporarily to his *fazenda*.

Her business affairs presented no difficulty. Lopes Matoso's fortune was tied up almost entirely in bonds and railway shares. As Lenita was the only child, there was no need for an inventory, much less a court ruling.

Colonel Barbosa's reply came swiftly — let her come, let her come at once! His old invalid wife was delirious with pleasure at the news that she was going to have a new companion, a young woman. No one lived with them but their only son, a middle-aged man, married, but who had been separated from his wife for many years — a keen shot and an eccentric, obsessed with himself and his books. In short, that she should not delay making preparations but be quick and tell him what day he should go to meet her.

A week later Lenita was installed in the *fazenda* of her father's old guardian. She had brought with her her piano, some artistic bronzes, a few curious knick-knacks and a quantity of books.

Chapter 2

At first, Lenita's loneliness on the *fazenda* was horrible, worse than in the city. The old woman, as well as being an invalid, was very deaf. Colonel Barbosa himself, a little younger than his octogenarian wife, suffered from rheumatism and at times kept to his bed for days on end. The divorced son had been away for months shooting in Paranapanema.

The work of the *fazenda* was managed by a *caboclo*[4] administrator, friendly enough but totally ignorant of anything which did not have to do with his work.

Lenita almost always ate on the huge veranda. After luncheon or dinner she would talk with the Colonel, and go to extraordinary lengths to make herself understood by the old woman, who, smiling and resigned, would cup her trembling hand round her ear to try to catch the words.

The girl soon tired of such entertainment and withdrew to her rooms to seek distraction in reading. She would pick up a book and put it down; pick up another and put it down. She found it impossible to read.

The memory of her father oppressed and constricted her soul, and everything reminded her of him — a passage he had marked with his nail in one book, a page turned down in another.

She would go out again to talk, go back to her rooms, go out once more — it was hellish.

The administrator's wife, affectionate in any case by nature, had received special instructions from the master with respect to Lenita. At all times of the day she would bring cups of warm milk, glasses of cane-juice, coffee, sweets, fruit.

Lenita sometimes refused these gifts, sometimes accepted them, indifferently, just to please the good woman.

Colonel Barbosa had given Lenita her own apartment — a large sitting room with two windows and a bedchamber. He had placed at her disposal for her personal needs a competent pale-skinned mulatto girl with a tall turban, as well as a smiling *caboclo* boy with very white teeth.

At times, Lenita spent hour after hour at the window, contemplating the buildings of the *fazenda*. This was situated halfway up a knoll, round the base of which ran a stream. The wide pastures stretched away in front. The monotony of light green was broken here and there by the dark patch of the thick foliage of a clump of *pau-d'alho*

---

[4] Caboclo — of mixed European and Amerindian descent.

trees, left intentionally to provide shade, and by the dirty yellow of the clumps of *sapé* grass. In the distance and to one side it was cut sharply by the virgin forest, dark, strongly marked, almost solid, its thousand colours blending into a single shade. The rolling land on the other side was covered by the cheerful, uniform, pale green of the cane-fields, waving ceaselessly in the wind. Further off the coffee bushes, in regular, unbroken rows, looked like a furry, blackish green carpet spread over the back of the hills. Here and there a bare patch of dark red ironstone soil marked a strident, deep crimson note, like dried blood.

And over it all arched the diaphanous, unblemished, silky blue of the sky in a festival of bright light, life-giving, intense…

When the weather broke, the countryside altered: the ashen sky, heavy with leaden clouds, seemed to lower as if wishing to smother the earth. The green surface lost its brilliance, grew dull and tarnished, drooped damply.

Lenita began to go out, to visit the surrounding area, now on foot, accompanied by the mulatto girl, now on horseback, followed by the lad.

But the exercise, the pure air, the freedom of life in the country did her no good.

A growing languor, a physical exhaustion, an almost complete prostration came over her whole being; she read nothing, the piano remained silent.

With the death of her father her nature seemed to have been transformed. She was no longer strong and masculine as she had been previously; she was afraid of being left alone and suffered sudden attacks of terror.

She would go to the invalid's room and collapse lazily in a chair, and there she would stay motionless for hours upon hours, barely replying to the Colonel's solicitous enquiries.

When she returned to her apartments, she would be seized on the way by an inexplicable anxiety and cling trembling to the mulatto girl.

She could not eat; she had a pitiful lack of interest in food, interrupted by violent whims for savoury or exotic dishes.

She suffered from constant salivation, almost uncontrollable bilious vomiting.

One morning she was unable to leave her bed.

The Colonel and the administrator's wife rushed to her bedside, insisting with the nurse that she should be given an infusion of lemon-balm or some household remedy while they awaited the arrival of the doctor, who had been summoned urgently.

When he arrived, Lenita was very low. Emaciated, pale, her eyes sunken in dark rings, she felt her chest constricted and struggled stertorously for breath. It seemed as if a ball were rising from her stomach to her throat, suffocating her. In the top of her head, a little to the left, she felt a narrow point of pain, fixed, stabbing, atrocious, as if her skull were pierced by a spike.

Her nervous system was highly irritated. The slightest noise, the shaft of light when the door was opened, wrung screams from her.

Doctor Guimarães, an oldish man with a kindly, intelligent face, approached the bedside; he examined the patient carefully and in silence without taking her pulse or inconveniencing her in the least, leaning low over her, his hands crossed behind his back, to hear her breathing, listen to her groans and observe the contractions of her face.

'When did this begin, Colonel?' he asked.

'She's been suffering ever since she arrived here, but she has never been like this until today.'

'Help, I can't breathe!' Lenita suddenly screamed out; twisting and turning she tore at her nightdress with both hands, scratching her breast. A sudden, vivid flush coloured her face, her eyes shone with a strange light.

'I know what this is,' said the doctor, 'it is an old acquaintance of mine. Don't worry, I'll be back in a moment.'

He left the room.

A few minutes later he reappeared, holding a Pravaz[5] syringe.

'Give me your arm, young lady. I am going to give you an injection and in a moment the pain will disappear.'

Lenita stretched out her bare arm with an effort; the doctor took it and began to pinch it slowly, deliberately, in a single spot at the level of the biceps. Then, holding the malaxated part between the finger and thumb of his left hand, with the right he inserted the needle of the instrument beneath the skin and, pressing down on the head of the plunger, injected the whole contents of the glass tube.

Lenita, despite the irritated state of her nerves, seemed not even to feel it.

---

[5] Charles Gabriel Pravaz, one of the inventors of the hypodermic syringe (1853).

The effect was immediate. Within a few moments her face lost its high colour, the nervous spasms of her limbs ceased, her eyes closed and a gentle sigh of relief swelled her breast.

She fell asleep.

'Leave her like that,' said the doctor. 'Let her sleep and she will be fine when she wakes. I will leave you a prescription also. In these cases I never fail to prescribe my potassium bromide.'

And they tiptoed out of the room, leaving the administrator's wife with Lenita.

Chapter 3

The doctor's prediction was fulfilled.

Lenita, after a long sleep, awoke calm, her nerves settled, her muscles relaxed and limber. But she was weak and depressed, complaining of a heavy head and a deep tiredness. She stayed in bed for two days, and was only able to get up on the third.

Her appetite returned little by little, she began to eat regular meals with enjoyment.

It would seem that she had only now begun to recover from the organic cataclysm of the death of her father.

Lenita felt that she had changed. She no longer had her old masculine tastes, and had lost her thirst for knowledge. She read the more sentimental of the books which she had brought: *Paul et Virginie*, the fourth book of the *Aeneid*, the seventh of *Telemaque*. The picaresque hunger of *Lázaro de Tormes* made her weep.

She felt a strange desire to devote herself to someone, no matter whom, to suffer for the sake of a sick person, an invalid. At times she remembered that if she married she would have children, little creatures dependent on her love, her care, her milk. Marriage no longer seemed impossible.

The image of her father began to fade in a haze of nostalgia which was still painful but now had its charm.

She spent hours and hours beside the invalid or talking to the Colonel; at times she laughed.

'That's better, much better!' said the kindly man. 'You should be more cheerful, my dear. You cannot change life — there's no use crying over spilt milk.'

One evening, finding herself alone in her sitting room, Lenita felt a delicious languor steal over her. She sat on the hammock, closed her eyes, and gave herself up to the gentle vertigo caused by its swinging.

Opposite her on a pier table, among other bronzes which she had brought, was one of Barbedienne's famous miniatures, of the statue by Agasias known as the *Gladiador Borghese*.

A dying ray from the setting sun, entering through a chink in the window, struck the statue directly, set it on fire, as if sending blood and life coursing through the dull bronze.

Lenita opened her eyes. The soft glow of the light reflected off the metal caught her attention.

She stood up, went over to the table, stared attentively at the statue: those arms, those legs, those bulging muscles, those knitted tendons, that strength and virility made a strange impression on her.

Dozens of times she had studied and admired this anatomical wonder in all its raw detail, in all the minutiae which make up artistic perfection, but never had she experienced such a feeling as now.

The bull-neck, the swelling biceps, the long thorax, the narrow pelvis, the retracted points of origin of the muscles in the statue, all seemed to correspond to a plastic ideal which had always been latent in her intellect, and which now awoke in a brutal revelation of its presence.

Lenita could not tear herself away; she was captivated, fascinated.

She felt herself weak, and took pride in her weakness. She was tormented by the desire of something unknown — indefinite, vague, but imperious and piercing. She divined that it would give her infinite pleasure if all the strength of the gladiator swooped down on her, treading her underfoot, bruising her, destroying her, tearing her to pieces.

And she yearned to devour with kisses the masculine lines stereotyped in the bronze, to clasp and merge into them. She suddenly blushed to the roots of her hair.

In a moment, by a sort of sudden intuition, she had learnt more about herself than in all her hours studying physiology. She saw that she, the superior woman, despite her powerful intellect, with all her learning, was no more than a simple female of the species, and that what she felt was desire, the organic need for the male.

She was overwhelmed by an immense despondency, an irresistible disgust at herself.

To strengthen her intellect through the blossoming of her reason, to study patiently, doggedly, at all hours of the day and night, almost every department of human knowledge, to accustom her brain to persist tirelessly in the subtle analysis of the most abstruse problems of higher mathematics — and then to fall suddenly, with Milton's archangels, from the heavenly heights to the muddy earth, to feel herself pricked by the goads of the *flesh*, spurred on to the concupiscence of animal heat, like a coarse negress, like a she-goat, like any animal … it was the supreme humiliation.

With a huge effort she threw off the maddening spell; swaying and supporting herself against the walls and furniture, she went into her chamber, closed the windows with difficulty and threw herself on the bed fully clothed.

For a long time she lay motionless.

A warm dampness spreading between her thighs made her start up suddenly, reacting violently against the lethargy which had prostrated her.

With trembling, nervous hands she threw off her shawl, quickly unbuttoned her bodice, tore open the ties of her black skirt and her petticoats and stood there in her shift. A wide patch of vermillion, glistening and vivid, stained the white cambric. It was the catamenial flood, the flow of blood of her fertility, which ran from her robust flanks as the ruby must spurts from the crushed grape.

More than a hundred times already nature had manifested itself in her in this way, but never had it caused her the same sensations as now.

When, at the age of fourteen, she had first experienced the phenomenon after feeling weak and exhausted all day, she had been panic-stricken, believing that she was mortally hurt, and had run screaming to her father, with the shamelessness of innocence, and told him everything.

Lopes Matoso had tried to calm her, saying that it was nothing; that it happened to all women; she should avoid damp, sun, the night air, and in three days, or five at the most, she would be better; and that she was not to be afraid when it recurred every month.

In time, her physiology books had completed her knowledge. In Püss she had learnt that menstruation is a sloughing of the epithelium of the uterus, occurring in sympathy with ovulation, and that the terrible and ill-famed flow is no more than a natural consequence of this sloughing.

She had resigned herself and become used to this imposition of her organism, as she had already become used to others. But just as a matter of self-study, she began to record the dates of its appearance with a red pencil mark in a little pocket calendar.

Night fell.

When the mulatto girl came to call her to dinner, she found her lying curled up, huddled in the bedclothes.

She asked if she was sick, and on learning that she was, went out and told the master. Then she brought her own blankets and pillows and made up a bed on the rug at the foot of the bed, where she stayed ready to be of service for whatever might be needed.

The Colonel, full of concern, came to the door of the bedroom to ask Lenita how she was.

It was nothing — she replied — just a minor indisposition of no consequence, and she would be fine when she woke the next day.

'My girl, you know I am your father now. If you need anything, be frank; have me called at any hour, don't be afraid to disturb me. My poor old wife is most upset, cursing the incapacity which makes her no use for anything. Wouldn't you like a cup of herb tea? A little hot wine?'

'Thank you, I don't want anything.'

'Very well, I'll leave you in peace. Until tomorrow. Try to sleep.'

And he went out.

Lenita fell asleep. At first she dozed fitfully, uneasily, waking with little cries. Then a sort of languor overcame her, a trance which was neither waking nor sleeping. She dreamt, or rather saw, the gladiator swelling on his pedestal, growing to the size of a man. He lowered his arms, straightened up, stepped down and walked to the bed; he stood at the bedside, contemplating her slowly, lovingly.

Lenita revelled in delight in the magnetic power of his gaze, as in the luxurious waters of a warm bath.

Sudden tremors ran through her limbs; her hair bristled in intense, lascivious arousal, at once painful and intensely pleasurable.

The gladiator reached out his left arm, leant on the bed, half sat, lifted the covers, and then, still looking at her with his fascinating smile, gently stretched out until he was lying touching her body with the provocative nakedness of his virile form.

His touch was not the cold, hard touch of a bronze statue; it was the warm, soft touch of a living man.

And at this touch Lenita felt an indefinable sensation sweep over her; it was at once fear and desire, terror and voluptuousness. She was eager but afraid.

The gladiator glued his lips to hers, his strong arms encircled her, his broad chest covered her delicate breast. Lenita was panting and shuddering with pleasure, but a pleasure that was incomplete, flawed, torturing. Embracing the phantom of her hallucination, she rolled like a wild beast in the heat of her rut.

Her nervous arousal, her erect tissue, her orgasm were manifested in every part — in the quivering of her swollen lips, in the nipples of her cupidinously taut breasts.

In a final convulsion she lost consciousness.

Chapter 4

Her return to health was plain to see.

She woke early, drank a cup of warm milk, went out for a walk in the fields, ate a healthy luncheon and then sat down at the piano where she played martial music *con brio*, cheerful, rousing pieces with bouncing rhythms.

She would go to the orchard where she ate the fruit and climbed in the trees.

She dined, supped and then went to bed, sleeping the night through.

She took on a new lease of life, frequently looking at herself in the mirror, adding saucy touches to her dress and putting brightly coloured flowers in her very black hair.

She used perfumes excessively; her linen reeked of vetiver, sandal, ixora, *peau d'Espagne*.

She ran and skipped, went for long rides on horseback, almost always at a gallop, urging the animal on with her crop or her hat, her face flushed, her eyes shining, her hair blowing in the wind.

She went out shooting.

One calm day after luncheon she took up the Galand shotgun which she habitually used, crossed the grass and took a shady track which crossed a broad tract of virgin jungle.

She went on a long, long way, distracted, self-absorbed.

Suddenly her ear was caught by the soft, monotonous murmuring of water away to her left.

As she was thirsty and wanted a drink, she turned in following a narrow trail.

She was brought up in astonishment by the majestic scenery which opened up before her a little way in.

At the end of a vast ravine rose a sheer wall of mossy black rock. Over it shot a jet of water, forming a small, crystal-clear lake, calm and deep, on the valley floor.

The water ran away noisily, tumbling in steps down the natural dam which closed the ravine's lower end.

The smooth surface of the lake mirrored the luxuriant vegetation which framed it.

Gigantic *perobas* with their dark foliage and wrinkled bark; ancient *jequitibás* spreading the green expanse of their cheerful crowns across the blue sky; white *figueiras* with their flattened roots spreading far out horizontally, their deformed branches like huge, maimed human limbs; spiny leafed *canchins*, dripping a caustic, poisonous sap from the fibres of their dark-red trunks; very tall, slender, smooth-trunked *guaratans*; pale *taiúvas*; blackish-green *pau d'alhos*, heavily luxuriant, foetid; dangerous *guaiapás*, sprouting sharp, poisonous spines; a thousand vines and creepers, a thousand different orchids with flowers of purple, yellow, blue, scarlet and white — all blended into multi-hued mass, an orgy of green, a debauch of colours, which overpowered and exhausted the imagination. The sun, darting shafts of light through the foliage, mottled the brown forest floor with greenish reflections.

Multi-coloured insects hummed or whirred in flight. The intermittent fluting of a *bronze sorocoá* drifted down from a *caneleira* tree.

A heady exhalation rose from the earth, blended strangely with the subtle fragrance of the scented orchids — and this mixture of the sweetest perfume with the rough odour of sappy roots relaxed the nerves and numbed the brain.

Lenita breathed deeply of this intoxicating atmosphere, surrendering herself to the spell of the forest.

She was overcome by a burning, irresistible desire to bathe in the cool water, to break the calm of the lake.

She turned every way, looked all round, to see if she might be observed.

'Nonsense!' she thought. 'The Colonel doesn't go out, the administrator and the slaves are working in the coffee plantation, there are no strangers at the *fazenda*. Besides, this isn't even a road. I am alone, absolutely alone.'

She laid down the shotgun, and beside it the broad-brimmed straw hat which she wore for protection on her excursions, and began to undress. She took off her short riding-habit and her whalebone bodice, then her black skirt and petticoats.

Standing in her shift, she lowered her head and raised her hands to the back of her neck to tie up her hair — and as she did so she gazed fondly under the white clothing at her firm, erect, satiny breasts, lined here and there with little blue veins.

And among the perfumes of the jungle she inhaled with delight her own odour, that young woman's pleasant smell which rose from her bust.

She sat on the ground, crossed her legs, unlaced her Clarks boots and pulled off her stockings; slowly and affectionately, she stroked her little feet where they were marked with the impress of the fine strands of Scottish wool. She stood up, quickly stepped out of her petticoats and with a little twist dropped her shift. The cambric collapsed in soft folds, covering her feet.

She was a beautiful woman.

Pale olive in complexion, she was tall and well-built; her arms and legs were rounded and muscular, her wrists and ankles fine, her hands and feet of aristocratic perfection, ending in shiny pink nails. Beneath the proud, jutting breasts her body tapered away to the waist, then broadened again into wide hips with a firm, softly swelling belly, shadowed at its base by the thick, dark pubescence. Her black hair with its bluish tints fell in a short fringe around her head and curled lasciviously down her neck, which was strong and well proportioned. She had a small head, lively black eyes, a straight nose and very white teeth between very red lips. On the left side of her face was a birthmark, a small, very dark, perfectly round spot.

Lenita contemplated herself with self-satisfied *amour-propre*, fascinated, entranced by her own flesh. She looked from herself to the lake and the jungle, as if to bring everything together to form a picture, a synthesis.

She squatted playfully on her heels, resting her right buttock on her right heel and crossing her arms on her raised left knee, in a pose resembling, reproducing the familiar position of the Salona statue of the *Venus Accroupie*.

There she stayed for a long while. Suddenly she leapt up, plunged into the water, surfaced and began to swim.

The lake was deep, but narrow. Lenita swam to and fro from one shore to the other, from the wall to the dam, the dam to the wall. She passed under the jet of water and shrieked with pleasure and alarm under the heavy pressure of the liquid mass on her smooth back.

She turned onto her back and let herself float, her legs stretched out, her stomach to the sky, her arms extended, slowly moving her open hands under the water.

She turned over once more and swam away again, swift as an arrow.

A shiver warned her that it was time to leave the water.

She stepped out with her body covered in goose-pimples, frozen and shivering. She sat in the sun in a clearing, waiting for her body to react to its warmth, twisting and shaking her loose hair. Her body gave off a subtle vapour, a tenuous aura, which enveloped her completely.

Before long, the heat of the sun and of her body dried her. She dressed, spread her still wet hair over her back, put on her hat, took up the shotgun and set off home at a run, humming a snatch of *Les Cloches de Corneville*.[6]

'Oh my sins!' exclaimed the Colonel when he saw her arrive, happy, smiling, her hair damp. 'If this crazy girl hasn't been for a swim in the pool under the cliff. The water there is icy… You must have caught a terrible cold!'

'All I've caught is a terrible appetite — I'll eat dinner for four today!'

'Hey, boy, go and fetch me the cognac bottle from in there, quickly.'

'Are you going to have a glass of cognac, Colonel?'

'You are going to have a glass of cognac.'

'I've never tried such a thing before.'

'Well, now you are going to try it; it is the only way I will forgive you.'

The cognac came, a genuine, old 1848 cognac. Lenita drank a small glass and choked. Her eyes watered. It was strong, but she liked it; she had another.

---

[6] Operetta by Robert Planquette first produced in France in 1877.

Chapter 5

The first day of the cane milling had arrived.

Already the previous day the blacks had been busy sweeping out the mill-house, washing the mill troughs and spouts, sanding and polishing the pans and the alembic with large quantities of lemon and ashes.

Dawn was barely breaking when a narrow discoloured strip could be seen in the green of the cane-field opposite, which gradually expanded, advancing lengthwise. The cutting had started. The white cotton clothes, the blue skirts of the female slaves, the red worsted shirts of the men, marked bright, vivid points in that ocean of pale green, swayed by hot gusts of wind.

In the mill-house, swept and clean, the four pans and the alembic of red, polished copper shone, reflecting the light which entered through the long windows. The furnaces stood at the end in the gloom, like great, gaping, greedy mouths.

The water, still held back in the channel, spurted through the joints of the sluice gate onto the paddles of the wheel in thin, crystalline jets. The rollers were clean and bright, the black grease on the axles and cogs gleamed. The long mill troughs and the huge cooler opened their wide mouths, the dark opacity of the much-washed wood absorbing the light.

In the distance, at first barely distinguishable but growing ever stronger, could be heard a continuous, high-pitched, monotonous, irritating squeal. The gang of blacks gathered in front of the mill sent up a wild shout, dancing in jubilation.

The first carts of cane were arriving.

Drawn heavily by slow, powerful, long-horned oxen, the vehicles crept forward, creaking and groaning under the enormous load of long, thick canes, streaked with green and purple.

Black drivers, tall and broad-shouldered, and with raw leather belts tied high round their waists, directed and spurred the ruminants with long goads, shouting ostentatiously:

'Hup, Lavarinto! Back, Ramalhete! Steady, Barroso!'

The carts entered the mill compound. Agile blacks jumped up onto them to start unloading. In a moment the canes, tied in bundles lashed with their leaves, were standing up in stacks.

Fire was lit in the furnaces under the pans; the sluice gate of the water channel was opened and the water began to fall violently onto the paddles of the wheel, which started to turn, slowly at first, then faster.

Cutting the ties of one of the bundles with swift strokes of his machete, the black working the mill began to feed the first canes between the revolving drums. There was a cracking sound of crushed fibres; white specks from the bagasse[7] which spewed out of the turning crushers spattered the dark housing; the cane-juice began to flow down the spout in a dull, greenish stream. After a short run, it fell into the big, surging, bubbling mill trough with its stiff, towering foam.

The black *bangüeiros*[8] with their long-handled skimmers took their places at the pans.

The cane-juice, flowing from a movable spout, filled them in an instant. The furnace glowed incandescent, radiating a gentle heat through the whole vast hall. The skilful skimmers tossed the smoking molasses through the air in golden streams, which fell back into the boiling, bubbling pans.

The air was filled with a sweet, sugary smell, alternating now and then with a tepid gust of rough human odour, the suffocating stink given off by the sweating blacks.

The Colonel enjoyed the work of the sugar crop. Overcoming his rheumatism, he spent the days of the cane milling sitting on a long, high mahogany bench fixed between two windows, not too close to the pans. He directed the work, checking the setting-point of the molasses in a very clean, well polished little copper cup, using a paddle to stir the sugar in the cooler when, after being poured into the copper stirring pans through a special moving spout, it collected there, its surface coalescing into a brittle, yellow crust.

Lenita never left the mill; she wanted to know everything, asked about everything.

The Colonel had to face a barrage of questions — in which months was the cane planted; how long did it take from planting to harvesting; when and how often did it have to be weeded; how was it cut; what was meant by *raising* or *lowering* the blade; what were the signs of ripeness; how could one tell overripe cane; what was *carimar*[9]; why did cane grown on well-worked soil have less vigorous growth and more sugar; how were the cuttings planted.

She went into the details of the process, made notes; she learnt that an *alqueire*[10] of farming land in the São Paulo district measured a

---

[7] The spent cane stalks after crushing.
[8] Whose job is to remove scum and impurities from the cane juice.
[9] A disease of sugar-cane
[10] A measure of area, 2.42 hectares.

hundred fathoms by fifty; that a quarter of that area, for the purposes of cane-farming, was called a *quartel*; that a *quartel* of suitable land in a good year yielded forty to fifty carts of cane; that a cart of good cane produced five *arrobas*[11] of sugar; that unrefined sugar free of clay sold for a better price than white sugar containing clay; that cow dung was a better replacement for clay.

She climbed up to the *tendal* where the moulds hung, two from each bar, and counted them; she calculated the sugar production of the four daily shifts; calculated what the sediment, scum and molasses would produce in cane spirit; estimated the capacity of the cases, the tanks, the big-bellied oak hogsheads; brought herself up to date with prices, comparing that year's with those of the previous nine of the decade; made generalizations and deductions, drew positive conclusions as to the income of the municipality in the near future, given the elimination of slave labour.

The Colonel was full of admiration. One day he said to her: 'I should have married a women like you. I'm not a poor man, but I'd be as rich as Croesus if had had you as my administrator since I started out. Even if I had a son or a grandson of your age to marry you…'

'Talking of sons, when is your son coming back from Paranapanema?' asked Lenita.

'How should I know? He's a special case, always was. Buries himself in his books and never comes out of his room for months. Then suddenly gets an urge and 'See you later!' off he goes to the wilds hunting, without a thought for anything else.'

'He's married, I think I heard.'

'Unfortunately.'

'Where's his wife?'

'At home in France.'

'Oh, so she's French then?'

'Yes. He married her in Paris, on a whim. By the end of the first year he couldn't stand her and she couldn't stand him. So they separated.'

'I didn't know your son had been in Europe.'

'Yes, he was there for ten years. When he came back he could hardly speak Portuguese.'

'Which countries did he visit?'

---

[11] A measure of weight, equivalent to approximately 15 kg.

'He went all over the place — Italy, Austria, Germany, France. He spent most time in England: he stayed there to study with a chap who says we are all monkeys.'

'Darwin?'

'That's right.'

'Then your son is a highly educated man?'

'Yes, he speaks several languages and knows quite a bit of science. He even knows medicine.'

'He must be very good company.'

'Indeed he is — at times. At others the devil himself couldn't put up with him. That's when he gets something which he calls… some odd English name.'

'Blue devils?'

'That must be it. So you speak some of the *roast-beef* language too?'

'I speak passable English.'

'Well then, when Manduca arrives, and if he's in the mood, you can practice your language to pass the time.'

'I will be very pleased to have a chance to practice.'

And from then on, despite herself, Lenita's thoughts turned constantly to this eccentric individual who, having lived for so long among the splendours of the old world, listening to the great names of science, studying at first hand the highest manifestations of the human spirit; who, having married one of the finest women in the world, a Parisian, had allowed himself to become so overwhelmed by boredom as to come and bury himself in a remote *fazenda* in the west of the province of São Paulo; and, as if that were not enough, went off to the unexplored jungle to hunt wild animals and live with uncivilised indians.

She knew that he was something over forty years old, only a little younger than her father when he died. She imagined him possessed of a robust virility which, if no longer youth, was not yet old age; she lent him a strong, athletic frame, that of the torso on the Belvedere; she saw him with deep, imperious, commanding black eyes. She longed to hear the news of his arrival; that he had already sent for the horses to bring him from the station to the *fazenda*.

And her happy state of mind continued to grow; she no longer felt grief at missing her father, only melancholy.

She drank cane-juice, but preferred chopped cane. She enjoyed sucking the cane, saying it was better than the juice; that the peeled cane, stripped with a knife and crushed between the teeth, had a special cool sweetness which it lost on being crushed between the rollers.

She loathed *furu-furu*, but she loved *ponto* or *puxa-puxa*.[12] When the molasses in the cooler began to thicken, developing a yellow skin, she would run her right index finger over the hot surface, gathering a thick gobbet which she licked with delight, smacking her lips, her eyes closed. One day, a negro whose job was to wheel the barrow with bagasse to the bagasse heap, and who had a heavy iron fetter fixed to his left leg, spoke to her:

'Missie, look at this leg of mine — all hurt. Iron very heavy. Speak with massah, get it taken off.'

And he showed her his ankle, covered in sores from the fetter, fetid, wrapped in dirty rags.

'What did you do to deserve this?'

'I sin Missie; I ran away.'

'Were you ill-treated? Were you afraid of being beaten?'

'No Missie; negro's good for nothin', is all; sometimes he loses his head.'

'If you promise me not to run away again, I will ask the Colonel to have the iron taken off.'

'I promise Missie; negro promise, God's word. You see. Saint Benedict will give Missie a husband, handsome as Missie self.'

And he gave a great foolish laugh.

Lenita smiled, amused by his wish for her, and the compliment.

Later she spoke to the Colonel — there was no reason for it, it was barbarous, an indescribable disgrace, he should order the iron to be taken off.

'Ah, my child! You don't know the rights and the wrongs of it. Barbarous? Nothing of the kind! There is a reason for everything in this world. This philanthropy business, this modern whining about abolition and equality and the devil knows what, it's all twaddle and humbug. It's as plain as can be — the black man needs the leather and the iron as he needs his mush and sacking. We'd soon see how far we'd get with the tilling if these people didn't have a good strap on the end of a stick, handled by a forthright overseer, to tickle up their backs when they're out in the field. I don't do and say these things because I am a bad man — indeed, I'm known for a good master. But

---

[12] Different sweet substances derived from sugar.

I have worked in the field and I know what's what. Well, just for you I'll have the iron taken off. But you mark my words, once that iron is off, he'll be away to the jungle.'

The harvest continued. Every day, more of the cane-fields were converted to stubble; the bright, pale green gave way to a sad, dirty, harsh brown. The wind swept over the dead, dry leaves, producing a rough rasping sound, a metallic crackling, which tried the nerves.

The bagasse heap grew and spread. The greenish white was dotted with the dark specks of the pigs, cattle and mules which spent the day there, chewing, masticating, ruminating. From time to time a violent scuffle would break out; high-pitched squeals were heard, mingled with hoarse lowing and fierce braying. A sidewise slash of the teeth, the toss of a horn, a couple of kicks had given victory to the strongest.

The sweet smell of the first pressings of cane-juice at the beginning of the harvest developed into a strong, dizzying odour of boiled sugar and fermented saccharine which could be smelt more than a mile away.

Chapter 6

The cane milling was over, and spring was well advanced.

The annual change of the seasons had rejuvenated the tropical forest; the shoots, the buds, the new fronds had burst into exuberance; here a pale, tender green, very delicate and velvety, there shiny as glass, with rusty tones, and elsewhere fiery red. In time, all would expand, gain strength, consolidate into strong, vigorous, healthy greenery.

Nature had put on new clothing — the season of love was upon her.

Florescence had burst out in all its luxuriance of shapes, its prodigality of shades, its extravagance of perfumes.

Over the dark coffee plantations she had drawn a soft, unvarying sheet of dazzling white corollas.

In the forest, every tree, every bush, every plant was filled with a strange energy.

Flowers in impossible abundance stretched out on the branches, jostling one another out of shape. They hung in limp, amorous voluptuousness, their calyxes down-turned, emptying waves of pollen, of dusty fecundity, into the air.

To the lasciviousness of the flora was added the erotic fury of the fauna.

Everywhere was heard the fluting and warbling, the howling and bellowing of love. The trilling of the *inambú*, the piping of the *macuco*, the squawk of the toucan, the throaty grating of the *jacu*, the clanging of the *araponga*,[13] the squeaking of the *serelepe*, the bellowing of deer, the plangent, almost human wailing of the felines.

Above this tempest of notes, this cataclysm of amorous groaning, could be heard the harsh growling of the *cachorro do mato*, and the piercing, frantic squeal of the *cará-cará* lost in the vastness.

The leaves shivered and shook, brushing and bruising one another. Brightly coloured insects, green as emeralds or red as rubies, clutched one another, trembling. Birds pursued one another in short, rapid, urgent flights, pecking and ruffling their feathers. Animals romped, chased and curvetted, their hackles erect. Snakes hissed softly to their mates, coiling lasciviously.

The hot, rough, electric emanations of the earth were wedded to the lubricious, humid warmth of the sunlight which filtered down through the foliage.

---

[13] Jungle birds. The *araponga* has a metallic call. The *serelepe* is a small mammal.

In every dark nook, every cranny in the rock, on the forest floor, on the stems of the grasses, on the branches of the trees, in the water, in the air, everywhere, muzzles, beaks, antennae, legs, wings sought and found one another, met and mingled in the heat of sexuality, the spasm of reproduction.

The air seemed to be split by lightning flashes of sensuality; all around one could sense warm gusts of voluptuousness. Above all other fragrances predominated the acrid, overpowering smell of seed, the odour of copulation, exciting and provocative.

Lenita was sunk in sloth. She would go out into the forest and when she found a patch of dry gravel, in deep shadow, she would lie down and settle herself comfortably on the thick carpet of dead leaves, surrendering to the erotic languor which emanated from the potent nuptials of the earth. When she went home she would stretch out in the hammock with her legs crossed, an unread book abandoned on her breast, her head flung back, eyes half closed; she would lie thus in a delightful languor for hours and hours.

Despite herself, she thought constantly, continuously of the eccentric hunter in Paranapanema; at every moment she saw him at her side, strong, athletic as she imagined him, conversing with her.

She had turned cruel. She pinched the black girls, and pricked animals which passed within her reach with a needle, or cut them with a penknife. Once a dog reacted and bit her. Another time she caught a canary which found its way into her room; she broke off its legs, dislocated one of its wings and released it, laughing with inward delight to see it flapping miserably with its one wing, dragging the other, resting its bleeding stumps on the muddy ground of the yard.

The slave whom she had had released from the leg-iron did indeed run away, as the Colonel had foreseen. One day he was brought back captive by two *caboclos*, tied with a rope round his upper arms.

There was no way out of it, said the Colonel, the man must be taught a proper lesson for having abused Lenita's generosity; he was going to have the iron put back on, and God Almighty would not get it taken off again.

Lenita intentionally did not intercede. She felt a burning curiosity to see the application of the *bacalhau*,[14] to witness at first hand this legendary, humiliating, atrociously ridiculous torture. She was highly delighted with this perhaps unique opportunity presented to

---

[14] Literally *codfish*, but this instrument of punishment will be described in detail below.

her, revelled in a strange, morbid voluptuousness at the idea of the contractions of agony, the screams of pain of the miserable negro, who not long before had aroused her compassion.

She was clever enough to find out from the Colonel in a roundabout way, without touching on the subject directly, that the punishment was to be administered in the trunk shed the next morning, at dawn.

She passed an uneasy night, waking at all hours, fearful that the heavy sleep of the early morning would cause her to miss the opportunity to see this spectacle to which she was so looking forward.

She rose early, while it was still very dark, and went out and across the yard, entering the orchard without being seen.

Its east side was closed by the row of slaves' quarters, the raw mud walls of which rose tall, blank, heavily cracked.

There was one house twice the size of any of the others: it was the trunk shed.

Lenita went over and leant against it, and drawing from her breast a little pair of scissors which she had brought, she began to bore a hole in the wall, at eye level, between two beams and two laths, at a favourable spot where a slightly loosened lump of mud already protruded, very stony and deeply cracked.

The scissors were short but solid and strong, of excellent steel, made by Rodgers.[15] Lenita warmed to her task, working enthusiastically, but patiently and skilfully. The steel bit into the friable mud and ground it away almost noiselessly. A dusting of yellowish powder stained the young woman's black dress.

The lump came away and fell inwards, hitting the soft floor of ill-beaten earth with a dull thud.

She was through.

Lenita leant back and froze, holding her breath.

After a few moments she stretched her neck forward and peered in. It was too dark for her to see anything inside. A loud, rhythmic breathing could be heard.

A long time passed.

The brilliance of the stars faded. A band of white light glimmered in the east, reddened, then flamed to purple with gleams of gold. The air grew thinner and subtler, and the birds burst into a chorus

---

[15] Joseph Rodgers was one of the best-known of the Sheffield cutlery makers in the nineteenth century.

— rough and ill-tuned, but cheerful, festive, titanic, saluting the new day which was breaking.

The loud ringing of the *fazenda* bell was heard.

Lenita peered in again; it was light in the trunk shed.

On one side stretched a wooden platform, polished to an oily gleam by the contact of dirty human bodies. The timbers of which it was made fitted into a solid mahogany balk, cut lengthwise into two pieces. These two pieces were juxtaposed, joined at one end by a strong hinge and held closed at the other by a bolt fitting. Rounded, semicircular grooves, cut out of the upper surface of the fixed piece, and the lower surface of the moving one, matched when the hinge was closed to make two round perforations some four inches in diameter.

This was the trunk.

The fugitive slave had spent the night lying on his back on the platform, his legs passed through the holes in the trunk just above the ankles, wrapped in a dirty, ragged old blanket of dark wool.

He was asleep, but awoke at the sound of the bell.

Grasping one knee with both hands, he sat up for a while, stretched, then lay back again, his limbs aching, resigned.

The door opened and the administrator came in, followed by one of the *caboclos* who had brought the slave in.

'Hey boss,' shouted the *caboclo*, 'look what I've brought you! *Chocolate, coffee, berimbau,*[16] *and the strap on the end of a bough*! You're getting fifty to break the habit of working on your own account. Don't you know that a negro who runs away is a disgrace to his master? Just look at my paintbrush — hear it ring, feel it sting!'

And he shook the *bacalhau* fiercely.

It is a sinister, vile, revolting instrument, but simple.

Take a strip of uncured leather three palms long, or a little more, and two fingers wide. Cut it lengthwise down the centre, but without separating the two straps at either end. Soak it well in water, then twist and stretch it and nail it to a board to dry. Once the leather has dried hard, fit a handle to one end, cut off the other, trim the two legs to sharp points with a penknife, and it is ready.

The administrator unbolted the trunk and the negro stood up pale, trembling and miserable.

His features seemed to dissolve from sheer terror.

---

[16] *berimbau*: a musical instrument, formed like a bow, of the Brazilian slave culture.

He fell to his knees, his hands clasped, fingers locked and knotted.

It was the ultimate expression of human abasement, of animal cowardice.

He made a horribly painful picture.

'For love of God, Mané Bento, Sir — I never run away again!'

He was weeping desperately.

'Don't make a fuss, boy,' replied the administrator. 'It's the Master's orders, and they have to be obeyed.'

'Call Massah!'

'The Master is in bed. He won't come — he can't. Cut the stories, drop your trousers and lie down.'

'Virgin Mary help me!'

'You didn't call on the Virgin when you tried to run away,' the *caboclo* called impatiently. 'Come on, get on with it and we'll get this over.'

The unfortunate looked around, as if seeking an opening to escape. Seeing none, he made up his mind.

Slowly, trembling terribly, he unbuttoned and dropped his dirty trousers, baring his buttocks, the typical hollow buttocks of a thin negro, already covered with gashes and criss-crossed with scars.

He bent his knees, placed his hands on the floor, stretched out and lay face down.

The *caboclo* took up a position to his left, measured the distance and leant forward; stepping back with his left foot, he raised the *bacalhau* and brought it down from to left to right, vigorously, swiftly, but without effort, with the science, the art, the elegance of a professional enthralled by his profession.

The two hard, inflexible straps made a metallic hiss, almost a whistling sound, the sharpened points flaying the epidermis.

Two whitish, powdery welts appeared on the purple skin of the right buttock.

The negro let out a fearful roar.

With measured rhythm the *bacalhau* rose, then hissed down, slashing and slicing.

The blood welled in drops at first, like liquid rubies, then flowed continuously, copiously, running down to the ground in streams.

The negro writhed like a wounded snake, digging his nails into the loose earth floor, beating with his head, screaming and howling.

'One! Two! Three! Five! Ten! Fifteen! Twenty! Twenty-five!'

The henchman paused for a moment, not to rest, he was not tired, but to prolong the pleasure, like a gourmet saving a *bonne bouche* for the end.

He jumped over the negro and took up a new position; the instrument hissed down from the other side and the punishment continued on the other buttock.

'One! Two! Three! Five! Ten! Fifteen! Twenty! Twenty-five!'

The howls of the slave were hoarse and strangled; his woolly hair was filthy with earth and plastered with sweat.

The *caboclo* threw the *bacalhau* down on the platform of the trunk and said:

'Now, a dash of salt to stop it going bad.'

And taking from the hands of the administrator a calabash which he had brought, he poured its contents over the lacerated flesh.

The negro started violently; a frightful, suffocated, inhuman bellow of pain burst from his throat. He lost consciousness.

Lenita felt a sort of spasm of pleasure, a vibrant thrill. She was pale, her eyes flashed, her limbs were trembling. Her lips curled in an icy, cruel smile, showing her very white teeth and pink gums.

The hissing of the whip, the screams and contractions of the victim, the sight of the running streams of blood intoxicated her, drove her to a demented frenzy in which she twisted her hands and beat a nervous rhythm with her feet.

She wanted, like the Roman vestals at the combats of the gladiators, to hold the power of life and death; she longed for the power to draw out the torture until the victim was exhausted; she desired to give the sign, *pollice verso*,[17] for the executioner to consummate his work.

And she trembled, shaken by a strange sensation, a piercing voluptuousness. There was a taste of blood in her mouth.

---

[17] Thumbs down.

Chapter 7

It had been raining continuously for almost a week. Water dripped from the soaking fronds of the joyous, luxuriant, shining forests. The thick, sodden carpet of dead leaves which covered the jungle floor disintegrated, reverted to humus. The bare earth of the roads grew green and slimy on the slopes and ramps, turned on the flat to water-logged, semi-liquid clay, rutted by the wheel-tracks of the carts, stirred, beaten and kneaded by the feet of the cattle; now swelled in pillows of mud, now hollowed into pools of dirty water, here yellow, there blood-red. The water rushed down the hillsides in boiling streams, chequered with froth; on the open plain, it spread in great, calm sheets, bathing the roots of the grasses.

The fields were swamp, the swamps, lakes.

The wet buds on the orange trees in the orchard hung limply. The exuberant new growth of the plum-trees, mangoes, peaches and cashews shone. The dark, lowering sky seemed to hang close over the earth.

The brimming stream frothed and gurgled.

Lenita, perched owl-like on her hammock, sitting cross-legged Chinese-style, spent most of the day reading, huddled in her shawl, cold, bored and ill-tempered.

At times she thought of the changes, the psycho-physical states through which she had passed while on the *fazenda*, where she had met no one of her own age, sex and education with whom she could share her feelings, who could understand her, advise her, strengthen her in this terrible battle of nerves.

She analysed the crisis of hysteria, the erotic fury, the access of cruelty which had seized her. She studied her present irritable, demoralizing depression, shot through with inexplicable whims. She often caught herself thinking involuntarily of the Colonel's son, this older, married man whom she had never seen; she felt her heart beat faster when he was mentioned in her presence. And she concluded that this was a pathological state, which threatened her with an incurable malady.

But then she thought again — she was not ill, her state was not pathological, it was physiological. What she felt was the spur of procreation, the imperious command of sexuality, the *voice of the flesh*, demanding from her its tribute of love, claiming its share of fecundity in the great work of the perpetuation of the species.

She thought of nymphomania, satyriasis, those horrors through which nature is revenged on women and men who violate her laws by observing an impossible chastity; she thought of the sacred horrors inspired in the Greeks and Romans by these *punishments of Venus.*

She imagined, as if through a mist, Greek nymphs of Dyctinna, Roman Vestals, odalisques converted from Christian families, pale, convulsive Christian nuns, biting their lips till they bled, eyes aflame, twisting and turning in their lonely cots in the forests; gnawing at themselves like maddened beasts, pricked by the goads of desire.

They filed before her, lubricious, alive, almost palpable — Pasiphae, Phaedra; Julia, Messalina, Theodora, Imperia; Lucrezia Borgia, Catherine of Russia.

One day the Colonel burst into her room.

'Great news! My boy is coming — well 'boy' is a manner of speaking. The old fellow, the hunter of Paranapanema.'

'Your son?'

'That's right. About time too, I was missing him.'

'But didn't he warn you, didn't he ask to be met…?'

'That's what I said. But that's him all over, scatter-brained. He can't and won't wait, can't abide delay. He hired horses in Rio Claro, he's on his way.'

'How did you hear?'

'A *caboclo* who left there early this morning; he's just been here.'

'And your son is out in this downpour?'

'That's water off a duck's back — he's used to it!'

'What time do you expect him to arrive?'

'It's six leagues from here. No doubt he set out after luncheon, at ten o'clock. The road is terrible, so it will take him six or seven hours. He should be here at four o'clock — five at the latest. Now tell me, would you prefer to have dinner at the usual hour or shall we wait for him?'

'Of course we should wait!'

The Colonel left the room.

Lenita quickly jumped down from the hammock. She ran to her bedchamber, combed her hair and put it up, fixing it on the crown of her head so as to look her best, leaving the whole back of her neck bare. She laced herself tightly and put on a high-necked merino dress, very simple but elegant. She put on earrings, a brooch, onyx bracelets, and very low-cut Louis XV slippers which showed off her black silk stockings, picked out with little white horse-shoes. On her left breast she pinned two pale, half open, strongly-perfumed roses.

'Bravo!' cried the Colonel enthusiastically when he saw her, 'Miss Lenita is pretty as a picture! It is just a pity that you are wasting candles on a dead sinner. The boy is not a boy, and what's worse, it's a dead end.'

Lenita blushed slightly and laughed.

'Come on, let's go in. I want my old lady to see you in this rig! Really, you're pretty enough to turn the head of Saint Anthony himself! That high black dress suits you to perfection. Indeed it does!'

It was almost dusk. The rain fell regularly in an unbroken downpour. Water gathered in pools in every depression in the yard; ran down all the slopes in floods, in torrents, in streams, in trickles.

On the top of the hill facing the house, down which ran the road, appeared two horsemen and a pack-horse.

Slowly, slipping at every step on the smooth, muddy road, they began to descend towards the *fazenda*.

The rain filled the air with a fine spray, bluring their outlines in a sort of ash-grey mist, streaked diagonally by the heavy, falling drops.

The Colonel saw them through the misted panes of a window.

'Here comes Manduca,' he said. 'Poor chap, he's soaked to the skin!'

Lenita, stopped the gentle rocking of her rocking chair, threw down the *Correio da Europa* which she was reading, dropped her arms onto her thighs, leant her head against the chair-back and sat quite still, very pale, almost fainting. The blood rushed to her irregularly pumping heart.

The travellers arrived.

They heard the tinkling sound of the horses shaking their bits nervously, then the heavy tramp of sopping, muddy boots, the dragging of spurs on the stone floor of the porch.

The Colonel hurried his stiff limbs to meet his son.

'What filthy weather!' said he, as he entered the ante-room, thumping his feet on the doorsill and taking off his rubber cloak, which he went to hang on a wooden hook. 'How do you do, Father? You're looking well. And Mother, still the same?'

'Everything as usual. How about you — good shooting? Health alright?'

'Splendid shooting — I'll tell you all about it. I'm in rattling good health, apart from this damned migraine which I can't shake off; it's torturing me horribly now. I'll go in and see Mother, then I'm off to my room — I suppose it's ready. Tell Amancio to bring me up a can of boiling water and a little mustard-powder, so I can have a hot mustard foot-bath.'

'You haven't had any dinner, and I don't suppose you had much luncheon. Eat something, it will do you good.'

'Eat! That's the last thing I want with this migraine.'

'What a shame! Lenita and I were waiting dinner for you...'

'Lenita? Who's Lenita?'

'She's the grand-daughter of my old friend Cunha Matoso, daughter of my ward, doctor Lopes Matoso, who died shortly after you went to Paranapanema. Didn't you get my letter telling you about it?'

'Yes, I did. I remember Lopes Matoso well. So his daughter is here now?'

'Yes, poor little thing. She couldn't stay in the city, she missed her father terribly. Come here, Lenita; come and meet my son, Manuel Barbosa.'

Lenita came out of the drawing-room, approached the new arrival and greeted him with a slight bow.

He pulled off his soaking hat and returned the salute.

'Your servant, Madam. Forgive me if I do not shake you by the hand, I'm filthy, covered in mud from head to foot.'

Manuel Barbosa was a tallish man, a little thin. The wet clothing clung to his body, accentuating its angular shape. His head was covered over with long hair, plastered flat and dripping with water, hiding his ears.

A growth of grizzled beard gave him an uncivilised, almost fierce appearance. With the migraine his complexion was pale, very pale, dull and ashen. He blinked repeatedly against the light. His drooping eyelids fluttered, and a mass of wrinkles like crows' feet ran away from the corners of his eyes.

Lenita, deeply disappointed, looked at him with pained curiosity.

'I deeply regret, Madam,' he continued, 'that you have waited dinner for me, and that my violent migraine will deprive me for today of the pleasure of your company. Pray excuse me.'

He passed on into the house, violently, brutally, jangling his spurs, his muddy boots leaving damp prints on the floor. The Colonel went after him.

Lenita retired to her room, slammed the windows, and refused dinner and supper. She answered the Colonel almost rudely when he insisted that she should go down and eat a piece of roast chicken, a slice of ham, some dessert at least.

She tore the two pretty roses from her breast, threw them on the floor and stamped on them, destroyed them. She undressed in a frenzy, impatiently tearing off buttons and bursting hooks.

She shook off her slippers, sending them flying with a swift, violent kick. She threw herself on the bed, curled into a ball, biting her arms, and burst into convulsive weeping.

For a long time she cried and sobbed. This crisis of nerves relieved her, calmed and settled her.

She began to reflect.

To conceive an ideal, she thought, to give it life as a mother gives life to a child, to form it, to dress it every day in new perfection; and suddenly to see reality impose itself, devastatingly prosaic, trivially brutal, brutally dull!

To imagine an idealised hunter out of Cooper,[18] a Nimrod, a 'mighty hunter before the Lord'[19], an athlete muscled like an ancient hero, and then to be met with a hang-dog individual, old, bedraggled, with uncut mane and grizzled beard, a groom, a boor who was barely polite to her!

And what was more, she would swear that he smelt of *cachaça*:[20] she had caught a whiff of it when he spoke to her.

But after all, what was this man to her? She had never talked with him, never seen him, never even heard of him until a short time ago.

For had she not, in her time, spurned the assiduous attentions of a cloud of aspirants?

And at this moment, from a certain perspective, was it not better as far as her heart was concerned? With no father, no mother, no brothers or sisters, emancipated, absolute mistress over herself, rich, beautiful, intelligent, cultivated, she had but to show herself in the city, or better still in São Paulo, in the court;[21] appear in society, garner admiration in order to queen it in sovereign style, to receive plaudits, to inhale to her heart's content the incense of flattery. Why insist on staying at the *fazenda*?

---

[18] James Fenimore Cooper, American writer b. 1789, was famous for his novels of the frontier, of which perhaps the best known is *The Last of the Mohicans*.
[19] Genesis 10. 9.
[20] Cane-based liquor, the typical spirit of Brazil.
[21] In Rio de Janeiro.

If it was the organic need of a man, the need to procreate which tortured her, why not choose from among the thousands a strong, sinewy, potent husband, capable of satisfying her, of satiating her?

And if one was not enough, why not stamp on ridiculous prejudice? Why not take ten, twenty, a hundred lovers, to kill desire in her, to exhaust the organism?

What did she care for society and its stupid moral conventions?

But Manuel Barbosa with his yellowish complexion, his blinking eyes, his uncut hair, his revolting beard, his wet clothing!

And the smell, the whiff of drink?

She would never forgive him; she hated him. She would have liked to slap him, to spit in his face.

It was nonsensical; to keep going back and harping on a vulgar creature, so common, who was not worthy of her hate, not worth thinking about.

She would return to the city... No, she would go to São Paulo and settle there for good; she would buy a big plot in an upper-class quarter, in Rua Alegre or Santa Efigênia, or in the Chá, and build an elegant town-house in the oriental style, graceful, decorated with fretwork. It would far surpass and outshine these mud-built barns, these impossible, enormous monstrosities, these dull, tasteless farm-buildings, with their mixture of styles, their faulty hygiene, lacking in charm and design. Ramos de Azevedo[22] would be in charge of the work, and the decorations and ornamentation would be by Aurélio de Figueiredo and Almeida Júnior. She would furnish it in polished black jacaranda, with matt carving. She would buy genuine Boule desks and side-tables in the sales in Paris, using an agent who knew his business. She would have tooled Cordova leather, Persian and Gobelin tapestries, *fukusas*[23] from Japan. On the pier tables, the *dunkerques*, in glass cases; in filigreed ironwood cabinets, in *étagères*, on the walls, everywhere she would scatter a generous profusion of porcelain — milky white or cream from China, in cheerful colours, subtle, but very vivid; scarlet and gold from Japan, magnificent, provocative, luxurious, fascinating; stoneware from Satzuma, artistic work, Arabian in style, almost European in the correctness of its design. She would seek out vases and plates of tender Sèvres, painted by Bouchet, Armand, Chavaux *père*, the two Sioux; she

---

[22] Engineer and architect b. 1851; built many fashionable houses in São Paulo in the late 19th century.
[23] Elaborately worked cloth used to cover a gift.

would contrast them with porcelain from the royal works in Berlin and the imperial factory in Vienna, the former royal blue, the latter blood-red tinged with rust; she would have a wealth of Saxe figurines, idealized, perfectly finished, delightful. She would feast her eyes on the oily patina of Japanese bronzes, on the absolutely real, human forms of Greek statues, on mathematical miniatures by Colas and Barbedienne. She would have marbles by Falconet, terracotas by Clodion, marvellous, ancient *netsukes*,[24] with microscopic filigree. She would look at herself in Venetian mirrors, keep her perfumes in little flasks of Bohemian cut glass. She would fill her jewel-cases and *vide-poches* with old jewellery, chrysolites and brilliants set in silver and old gold reliquaries from Oporto.

She would have expensive horses; she would ride to Ponte Grande, to Penha, to Vila Mariana in an unrivalled Parisian *huit-ressorts*, drawn by enormous, mettlesome, pure-blooded Frisians, with very fine, dark coats.

She would become famous for her tremendously elegant, but *risqué*, even scandalous, toilettes.

She would travel all over Europe, spend a summer in St Petersburg, a winter in Nice, she would climb the Jungfrau and gamble in Monte Carlo.

Then she would return, give banquets; she must shock palates, accustomed to pork loin and mince made from yesterday's meat, by giving them smoked herrings, caviar, partridge *faisandée*, whole roasted larks, all the thousand subtle gastronomic inventions of the Old World; her guests would drink Johannisberg, Tokai, Costanza, Lacrima Christi, Château d'Yquem, all the delicious, expensive wines.

She would have lovers — why not? What did she care for the murmurings, the 'Have you heard…?' of hypocritical, scandal-mongering Brazilian society. She was a rich, sensual young woman — she would take her pleasure. If people wanted to be scandalised, let them.

Then, when she grew older, when she wanted to become respectable and live like anyone else, she would marry. It was so easy; she had money, she wouldn't lack for aspirants, educated men who would acquiesce in the appearance of marriage which she would impose on them at her fancy. It was only a question of asking, of choosing.

---

[24] Japanese miniature hand-carved sculptures.

Chapter 8

The rain had stopped, the weather was magnificent. The white sunlight filtered down through the fine air from the blue, cloudless sky. Nature expanded happily like an invalid returning to life, a convalescent.

Lenita rose in good health, but bored and irritated. The memory of Manuel Barbosa tortured her. To have to meet him every minute of the day, at table, in the drawing room, walking about the house and the yard; to see him lounging, rocking in the rocking-chairs, with his mane of hair, his grizzled beard… it was horrible.

When she was called in for luncheon she went reluctantly, in an evil temper. She had tied her hair back carelessly, wrapped herself negligently in a shawl, left off her stays, had not even laced herself. She was wearing sandals.

As she went onto the veranda she kept her eyes on the floor, determined not to face her disagreeable companion.

The colonel was at the table.

'Good morning Lenita; so how do you feel? Very disappointed with the boy, eh? Well, he's gone one better! He went into town early this morning. Had urgent business to attend to — at least, that's what he said. He appeared and left immediately. His migraine is like that; it torments him to desperation, but an hour or two of sleep and it goes without a trace.

'I'm so glad he is recovered,' replied Lenita dryly; to herself she thought: 'I hope one day he goes to sleep and never wakes up! The best thing an animal like that can do is to die, to disappear. The world belongs to strength and beauty, because in the end beauty is strength. And that beard! The devil take him, beard and all!'

And she was delighted that for that day at least she would not have to see and suffer Manuel Barbosa.

Moreover, she had decided that she would not stay on the *fazenda* any longer, but would return to the city, and from there to São Paulo.

She enjoyed her luncheon, played the piano for a while, then went out for a long walk before dinner. She only thought about Manuel Barbosa two or three times, with less indignation now, without resentment, almost with indifference. She thought herself merely ridiculous for having made a hero of him in a long access of extravagant hysteria. He was a poor devil, a bumpkin, past his best, in declining health. He hunted for the sake of it, without poetic intuition, like a beast, like any *caboclo*. He drank *cachaça*. It was true that he had been to Europe, but having been in Europe did not change a man's character. He was what she should have expected him to be — an uninspiring, common fellow, below average even.

In the evening she retired to her rooms and began to pack her bronzes, her marble and porcelain *bibelots*. She wrapped them carefully and lovingly in tissue paper, arranging them in the bottom of a huge American trunk which she had brought, fitting them together, protecting them with wrappings of old newspaper, with napkins, linen and small clothes. She took the meticulous care of a mother or a passionate enthusiast. At moments she forgot herself in the rapt contemplation of a little *sêvres* jar, a marvellous statue, so carried away that she would kiss them.

Very late that night, when she was already in bed, she heard the clatter of horses, footsteps, the jingling of spurs.

'There, that brute's arrived,' she said to herself, and her thoughts returned to her early departure for the city, and thence to São Paulo.

The weather had settled. The clear, cold, starry night gave way to another bright, sunny day.

Lenita rose very early, drank a cup of milk and went out for a walk in the pasture. On her way back she turned into the orchard to see the newly-formed figs, the pliable tendrils of the vines.

From a *cravo* orange tree, its dense, spreading foliage growing from ground level, she heard the cheerful call of a *tico tico*.

'It's got a nest,' thought Lenita, and she began to look for it, opening and pushing aside the twigs.

She stopped, sniffing the air. There was a pleasant smell of Legrand soap and Havana cheroot.

She walked round the orange tree and came face to face with Manuel Barbosa coming towards her, smiling, with a slight courtly bow, holding his hat in his right hand and in his left a splendid, scented, red carnation.

A tenuous curl of bluish smoke rose from the cheroot which he had thrown down.

Lenita stopped, confused and surprised, uncertain what to think.

The man before her was not the Barbosa of the other evening; this was a transformation — a gentleman in every sense of the word.

The high, smooth crown of his narrow head was bare, with a very white band showing at the base of the hair. This had been cut half length, and was plastered in an elegant curve over his forehead in the style of Capoul,[25] highlighted by its many silver strands. His face was absolutely regular, and he was very cleanly shaven. The pallor of the other evening had been replaced by the healthily bronzed complexion of a fair-skinned man burnt by the sun. His mouth, pure Saxon, surmounted by well-trimmed pepper-and-salt moustache, opened in a frank, friendly smile to show very clean, strong, regular teeth. He was slimly built, with delicate feet and well-formed, well-manicured hands.

He was wearing a loose, pale cashmere suit, a cream cravat, a dazzlingly white shirt with a turn-down collar which showed all the strength of his powerful neck. In the button-hole of his jacket was a scented, many-petalled rose.

He approached Lenita with polite grace.

'Madam, you must have formed a very poor impression of me the day before yesterday. When I have migraine, I cease to be a man — I become a bear, a hippopotamus! Would you do me the honour of accepting this carnation? Come, allow me — I am an old man, I could be your father.'

And with easy familiarity he fixed the flower in her hair.

Then, stepping back a couple of paces, he looked at her with the air of a connoisseur, his head on one side, and said:

'How well the bright red goes with your dark hair. You are very lovely.'

The look which shone between his half-closed lids was so gentle, so paternal, his speech so smooth, that Lenita did not take offence, or reprimand his audacious remark. She smiled and asked:

'Are you fully recovered now? You are not tired from your journey? Have you no after-effects from your migraine?'

'Oh no! I am not tired by travelling, and when my migraine goes, it goes completely. May I offer you my arm? Shall we take a turn round the orchard before luncheon?'

Lenita accepted.

In an instant, as if by electricity, her feelings had changed. To the yearning for the ideal man of her hysterical fixation, to the dislike of the real man of the evening before last, seen in such unfavourable circumstances, there had succeeded, here and now, a sudden, calm, good-natured affection, which attached her, subjugated her to Barbosa. She found in him a superior *bonhomie*, a communicative familiarity, which reminded her of her father.

---

[25] Joseph Capoul, b. 1839; famous French tenor.

They talked at length as they walked. Principally they spoke of botany. Barbosa established a detailed contrast between the flora of the Old World and the New; he gave technical descriptions and went into the minutiae of his own personal observations. He compared the mathematical succession of the seasons in Europe to the monotonous magnificence of the eternal springtime of Brazil; pointed out that the dominant characteristic of the forests there was mono-culture — forests consisting only of oaks or chestnuts or poplars — while here a hundred families intermingled and elbowed one another, so diverse that often one would not find two individuals of the same species within a radius of a thousand metres. He made an exception for the *Araucaria brasilensis* in the regions of Minas and Paraná, and again for the tropical palm-trees, which he said were legion. Lenita followed him with deep interest, displaying her own profound knowledge of the subject, asking well-informed questions. She quoted Garcia d'Orta, Brotero and Martius, criticised Correia de Melo and Caminhoá, confessed herself a sectarian when it came to species, and an ardent follower of Darwin, whose opinions lay at the root of their mutual esteem; by the time they went in for luncheon, they were old friends.

'Hello!' said the Colonel from the door, seeing them arrive arm in arm. 'A very good day to you! To the devil with sadness! So you've made friends, as I expected. But come in, come in, this isn't the moment — luncheon is getting cold, it's been on the table for half-an-hour.'

'Yes, Father. Miss Helena has been a surprise to me — a revelation. I knew that she was very well-educated, but I thought that meant well-educated in the way of girls in general, especially in Brazil — piano, singing, four fingers of French, two of English, two of geography and… that's that! But I was mistaken; Miss Helena is astonishingly erudite, indeed, she has the true scientific spirit. She possesses a superior mind, admirably cultivated.'

'Sir, you are far too kind!' returned Lenita, visibly satisfied.

'Now listen to me, that's enough of these *Sirs* and *Misses*. You are Lenita and Manduca, and there's an end to it! Ceremony is only for church; it gets on my nerves and brings on my rheumatism! Now, let's have luncheon.'

From that day on, Lenita and Barbosa were inseparable. They read together, studied together, walked together and played duets on the piano.

In the Colonel's saloon they set up an electro-physics study.

The old room with its bowed, bare walls, was filled, quite out of character, with the most modern scientific instruments, in which the shiny yellow of the varnished metal casing harmonised with the dark tone of the black lacquered parts, the crystalline transparency of the variously shaped glass tubes, the sheen of the polished wood supports and the fresh green silk of the coils.

Enormous Leyden jars were grouped in formidable arrays; there were Ramsden and Holtz machines, Cruikshank's and Wollaston's voltaic piles, Grove's, Daniell's and Leclanché's batteries, elegantly finished potassium chromate cells, Planté's accumulators, Ruhmkorff coils, Geissler tubes, Foucault and Duboscq regulators, Jablochkoff candles, Edison lamps, telephones, telegraphs. Fascinating shapes protruded in every direction, with their matt, diaphanous or reflective surfaces which at once absorbed, refracted and reverberated the light in a thousand different ways.

The current hummed, showers of bluish sparks popped on all sides with sharp cracks, bells rang and jingled.

An acrid, pungent, irritating odour filled the air, of nitric acid and ozone.

Barbosa and Lenita, engrossed, intoxicated by their experiments, exchanged rapid, almost abrasive words, like two long-standing colleagues, giving one another brief, imperious commands. Suddenly, one or other of them would stamp a foot, suffer a facial spasm, clench a fist or shake an arm: a moment's carelessness had been punished by an immediate shock. The Colonel watched from the door.

His saloon had been converted into a den of witchcraft, he said, and at any moment a thunderbolt would come and blow all this hocus-pocus to kingdom come.

He refused the insistent invitations of Lenita and his son to come and observe close-to the luminous effects of electricity in a vacuum, the brilliant colours produced in the Geissler tubes, saying that he would not go in for an act of parliament, and that he had been put off any desire to investigate electricity for the rest of his blessed life by two shocks which he had once suffered in the telegraph station.

To the observation that electricity might be useful as a cure for his rheumatism, he replied that anyone who wished might be cured with such medicine, but not he.

Once Lenita's scientific curiosity about electricity — which she had previously only learnt in theory — had been satisfied by experimental studies, they passed on to chemistry and physiology. Then they went on to linguistics and languages, especially Greek and Latin. They translated from Epicurus's Fragments, or from Lucretius's *De Natura Rerum*.

In their studies, and in the conversations which were an extension of their studies, on walks and excursions in the country, the time flew by. They rose very early and stretched their evenings till late. Once, when the boy went for the mail, he brought Barbosa a lacquered volume. It was an exposition by Viana de Lima of the evolutionary theories of Darwin and Haeckel. Lenita was wild with delight with this new work written in French by a Brazilian. They began reading after supper, read on into the night, and were so enthralled that they were surprised by daybreak.

It was only when the candles dimmed in the first light of dawn that they came to themselves. They laughed and laughed, then retired disappointed to their rooms, but could not sleep. They reappeared for luncheon and took up their reading again.

That night, after saying goodnight to Barbosa and going to her room, Lenita concentrated as she undressed, reflecting on her state of mind. She discovered that she was happy, found in herself gentle feelings for all that surrounded her, and that she was seeing life through a new prism. She felt, with a pang of remorse, that she was forgetting her father. The rest of the night, until she should see Barbosa again, seemed interminable.

She lay down, made herself comfortable and tried to compose her mind for slumber, repelling the confused ideas which came to her. She fell asleep.

Early, very early, at cock-crow, she awoke, her heart full of joy. She got up at once, brushed her teeth carefully and proudly inspected them in the mirror, shining the light into her mouth, pulling the lips away to look at the gums. She washed her upper body at length with cold water to freshen her skin, moistened and perfumed her hair with violet water and combed it carefully. She changed her nightdress for a fine, open-work cambric shift, laced her stays, and dressed jauntily. She trimmed, filed, smoothed, varnished and polished her nails.

And through all this she thought of Barbosa, anticipating the pleasure of the moment when she would see him, hear his voice in a cheerful, affectionate 'Good morning', shake his hand, feel the warmth of his contact.

Barbosa was no longer a boy, he did not sleep very long — a few hours were sufficient.

He lay down, tried to read, but could not. The image of Lenita interposed itself between his eye and the printed page. He saw her at his side, became absorbed in this semi-hallucinatory contemplation, spoke aloud to her, gripped his book or newspaper desperately; he stretched, tossed and turned, went to sleep, woke again, struck a match, looked at his watch, saw it was still night-time, went back to sleep, woke once more, and so on until day broke and it was time to get up.

'I don't know what this is,' he thought. Admiration for real talent in a girl, for unequalled superiority of abilities in a woman? Possibly. But in Paris he had long worked with Mme. Brunet, the extremely learned translator of Huxley; with her he had carried out hundreds of anatomical dissections and gone deeply into embryology. He respected her, admired her, but he had never felt with her what he felt for Lenita. And it was not that Mme. Brunet was ugly, quite the reverse. No, this was not simple admiration. But what the devil was it then? Genuine love, with a definite carnal object, did not describe it either; at Lenita's feet he had never yet felt a lascivious desire, had not suffered the pricking of the goad of the flesh. He had once felt a passion which had brought him to the ultimate folly of marriage, but that had passed; indeed, he was divorced from the wife to whose temper he had been unable to adapt. He was chaste up to a point, only seeking sexual relations when the physiological demands of his male organism made themselves felt, imperious, threatening his health. He attached no more importance to this than to the exercise of any function, the satisfaction of a simple organic need. But what then were his feelings for Lenita? It was not friendship in the strict sense of the word — such as a man feels for a man, or even a woman for a woman. Friendship is impossible between two people of opposite sexes unless they have lost all characteristics of sexuality. Ideal, romantic, platonic love? It must be that. But how ridiculous, great God, how immeasurably ridiculous! Sentimental languishing in his forties, when the hardening of the brain no longer permits fantasy, when the struggle for life has killed illusions!

The fact was that he had to be near her; that it was only in her presence that he came alive, thought, studied, that he was a man. He was a prisoner, reduced to nothingness.

Chapter 9

A major commission house had gone bankrupt in Santos. As a result, the Colonel had lost nearly thirty *contos*.[26]

'That trading centre was a *Caco's Cave*, a Calabria!'[27] said he, on hearing the news one morning. They were bleeding the plantation-owner dry; mixing the good coffee, which he sent, with the sweepings and with second grade beans bought on the cheap; and they called this honest dealing *cramming* or *making bulk* — and they were absolutely right because they were cramming themselves with money, a huge bulk of looted cash! They rendered sales accounts to the landowner as and when they felt like it and the accounts themselves might as well have been in Greek when one came to try to check them. Everyone ate at the landowner's expense — the agents, the railway companies with their excessive tariffs, the government with its old and new taxes, the carters' associations; the commission houses ate three times over, the address agents — the drones! — the export agents, everyone! And finally, to cap it all, to spirit away what little money was left, along came the holy remedy of bankruptcy — *casual* bankruptcy of course, because where there are expert book-keepers nobody ever goes bankrupt fraudulently!

It was decided that Barbosa would leave the next day for Santos, to see if he could salvage something from the wreck. So after luncheon he had a long talk with his father, discussing, calculating, drawing up conditions, laying the basis for negotiation. Then he mounted and rode off to the *fazenda* of their nearest neighbour, Major Silva, with whom he needed to talk the matter over as he too had an interest in the business.

When she said good-bye to Barbosa, Lenita felt as if she had stepped into an immense vacuum, although she knew that he would only be absent until the evening.

The idea of another absence in the future, of his journey to Santos, tortured her.

As a palliative for her pain, she determined to pack Barbosa's trunk herself, on the pretext that it would not be done properly by the careless hands of a slave.

Following the chambermaid who was responsible for his linen, she entered Barbosa's room for the first time.

---

[26] A *conto* is strictly speaking one thousand, but as the debased currency was generally referred to in *mil-reis* (thousand reals — c.f. introduction and ch. 10) a *conto* in fact represents one million

[27] *Caco* was a legendary Spanish robber-giant who stored his ill-gotten gains in his cave. The region of Calabria in Italy was once notorious for its brigands.

At the end of the room stood a narrow bachelor's bed, neatly made, with gleaming white sheets and pillow-cases. Beside the bed-head stood a marble-topped night-stand, and on it a pewter candle-stick with the stump of a tallow candle, together with a silver match-box and an issue of the *Diário Mercantil*; close to hand stood a vast table covered with green baize, with a few books, writing materials, two revolvers, a Japanese dagger and a photograph of Sarah Bernhardt. At the foot of the bed was a many-armed clothes stand. On the walls, in the spaces left between the washstand and a huge chest-of-drawers, were bottles covered in wickerwork, machetes, fine quality arms for hunting and target-shooting, muzzle-loaders, breech-loaders and repeaters, shipped by Pieper, Habermann, Greener, Fruwirth. A wardrobe, an easy chair and a few ordinary chairs completed the furnishings.

On entering, Lenita felt herself overwhelmed by an unaccountable embarrassment. Her sense of shame revolted, she seemed to breathe indecency in this male room. Her chest felt constricted, she coloured, and her voice trembled as she asked the maid for Barbosa's linen.

The maid opened a chest-of-drawers. She took out starched white shirts, soft flannel night-shirts, clean white linen underpants, towels, white and Brittany linen stocks, coloured silk scarves, Scottish woollen stockings, and piled them on the bed.

She went to fetch a big English trunk with a flexible expanding section and stood it beside the bed. A stained label with the words 'Tamar, cabin' made a splash of colour on the black leather. She unbuckled the straps and opened the two halves.

Lenita lined one of the two compartments with a towel of finest cotton from the Minas region, fringed with open-work; and with that meticulous care, that manner peculiar to young girls, she began to stack one piece on another, perfuming each with a puff of Victoria scent spray.

The blood red and royal blue of the silk scarves, the dark gold, bottle green and lustrous black of the Scottish woollen stockings stood out in crude contrast against the white of the linen.

The maid went out to another room to fetch some cashmere suits which Barbosa had told her that he wanted to take.

Lenita was left alone. She went to take the last shirt from the bed and noticed that there was a barely visible indentation in the material of the bedspread, and a deeper depression in the embroidered pillow.

Clearly, after the bed had been made, Barbosa had stretched out for a rest.

Impelled unconsciously, automatically, by a nervous attraction, Lenita laid her hands on the thick bedspread, leant over and put her head close to the pillow.

The pleasant, animal smell of a healthy, clean human body rose from the pillow, mixed with a slight aroma of *Eau de Lubin*.

As she inhaled this subtle emanation, Lenita felt a sort of electric tremor run through her organism; she was tormented by a vague desire, a thirst for sensations. Almost in a swoon, she fell face down onto the bed, buried her face in the pillow, drawing in the virile odour in short, urgent gulps as she brushed and rubbed her breasts against the rough, white fustian of the bedspread.

Her sensations were almost the same as on the night of her hallucination with the gladiator — a terrible, mordant, delirious pleasure, with strange sympathetic repercussions, but incomplete, flawed.

She gripped the cambric of the pillow with her teeth, moaning and whimpering in spasmodic contractions.

'Eh-ah!' cried the maid, entering at that moment. 'Missie having an attack!' And throwing the clothes which she was carrying onto a chair, she ran to Lenita, took her up in her arms and shook her violently.

Lenita calmed herself immediately. She was pale and trembling; her eyes were shining, her mouth was dry and she could hardly speak.

'No... it's nothing,' she said, 'a dizzy spell. I'm all right now. Fetch me a glass of water.'

'Missie,' said the maid pensively, 'it was the strong smell from the bottle you were putting on the clothes made you feel bad. It made me dizzy too. You be careful.'

And she went out

That evening, when Barbosa returned from Major Silva's *fazenda*, he found Lenita changed. She did not seek his company or address him, barely responding to his many and repeated questions.

Unusually, she retired to bed early, before dinner, saying that she felt unwell.

Barbosa said his farewells to his mother and father. He had no wish to wake them early in the morning, and he planned to leave before dawn.

He went to his room, but could not sleep. The journey which lay before him annoyed him intensely. He did not know how he would cope with being away from Lenita. The few hours he had spent at Major Silva's *fazenda* had seemed an eternity. He had returned at a gallop, and then to cap it all he had been met with her strange behaviour.

He finished packing his trunk.

'Well really,' he said to himself, 'Marciana has done an excellent job. It's beautifully done, with taste even, artistically. But where the devil did she get the Victoria scent from? It smells delicious. She deserves a tip — and she shall have it.'

He pulled a bottle of cognac from the wardrobe, drank off a glass and lit a cheroot.

He began to reflect.

What was the matter with Lenita? Could she have fallen ill so suddenly? Her period — that was it, for certain. As Van Helmont says so rightly: *tota mulier in utero*.[28] But surely he wasn't in love with the girl? What a joke!

He drew hard on his cheroot, his thoughts marched on.

He was married; he was almost an old man. Where would this lead…? He was not so fatuous as to believe that the girl could also be in love with his respectable person… but after all, why not? Many an old man had inspired passions. Lesseps's[29] wife was a young girl, almost a child, and married him for love. And besides, he, Barbosa, was not old; he was mature, nothing more. But if what existed between him and Lenita was not — could not be — mere comradely affection, simple mutual esteem, what was he to do? He could not marry her, he was married already. Take her as his mistress? Of course not! He held no deep prejudices; for him marriage was a selfish, hypocritical, profoundly immoral and supremely stupid institution. But still, it was an institution which had existed for thousands of years, and there is nothing more dangerous than to defy, to crash headlong into old institutions; they must fall, indeed, but in their own time, as slowly as they were formed, not with a crash, a lightning stroke. Society stigmatized free love, love outside marriage; there was nothing for it but to accept the unnatural decree of society. Besides, his father

---

[28] 'All of a woman is in her uterus.' Jan Baptist van Helmont (1577–1644) Flemish scientist and doctor.
[29] Ferdinand de Lesseps, builder of the Suez Canal, entered on his second marriage at the age of 65.

looked on Lopes Matoso as a son, and on Lenita as a grand-daughter. A scandal would wound him deeply, and perhaps kill him.

He sat down at the table, knocked the ash off his cheroot into an ashtray, leant his left elbow on his left knee and the side of his head on the palm of his hand; he became lost in thought, inhaling one draught of smoke after another.

After a long while he stood up, threw away the butt of his cheroot and began to pace nervously to and fro.

'No!' he exclaimed finally. 'There must be an end to this, it can't go on.'

He went to bed.

At three o'clock he got up, without having slept, called his servant and ordered him to saddle the horses, then washed and dressed. He pulled on boots and gloves, put on his riding coat and hat, gulped down a cup of coffee brought by a negress; then went out, mounted his horse, and set out on his journey, with his servant following.

Lenita had not slept either.

The human, masculine smell which she had breathed on Barbosa's pillow was nothing less than poison to her nerves. She felt herself prisoner once more to her old hysterical nausea. She felt longing, desire — but this longing and desire were stronger and had a clear object. Her longing, her desire, were for Barbosa.

He had materialised before her eyes, taken on new proportions, realized her ideal. She had allowed herself to be subjugated, dominated, by his robust, sinewy physique, his penetrating, cultivated mentality.

The haughty, proud female, conscious of her own superiority, had found a male worthy of her, the mistress had become slave.

Hearing the clatter of the departing horses, Lenita opened the window, raised the sash, and her eyes followed the forms of the two riders as they faded into the early morning mist.

She saw them stop; the rider who went ahead turned round, his pale riding coat marking a white spot in the gloom of the morning.

Did they stop for one of the thousand little incidents of the journey? Or was it for Barbosa to look once more on the house which held her? Was it a farewell?

Unconsciously, without thinking, Lenita bunched her fingers, raised them to her lips and blew a kiss into space.

Disoriented, her breast on fire, although she was quite sure that no one had seen her, she closed the window, threw herself on the bed and burst into convulsive sobs.

The sun rose, bringing a beautiful, radiant day.

Lenita got up, dressed hurriedly and went out to walk round the orchard, leaving the glass of milk and the cup of coffee which the servant had brought her untouched.

The fine air of the cloudless morning, saturated with the balmy scents of the trees, stifled, suffocated her — it was like breathing lead.

The sunlight gilding the soft green of the fields appeared crude and unfamiliar to her eyes. The vegetation, her whole surroundings, seemed somehow hostile.

The stillness of the neighbouring hills and the mountains visible in the distance was hateful to her. An earthquake, a cataclysm to lay low the hills and raise the valleys, spilling the rivers and convulsing the whole world, would be much better matched to her state of mind than this stupid, barbaric calmness of nature.

She imagined herself encircled by high walls of burnished steel, which were constantly closing in on her. Everything spoke to her, reminded her of Barbosa.

Here was the orange tree where she had encountered him like an avatar; smiling, open, communicative, as if transfigured into the guise which had captivated her in an instant.

There was a group of plum trees which had served as matter for a lecture on industrial botany. She remembered well — *Indian Plum, Canadian Plum* — inappropriate names, false origins. The tree was native to China and Japan, where it grows wild: Eriobotria, *Mespilus japonica*. It would have a great future when the country became industrialised. The jam it produced was unmatched, and the liqueur, twice distilled, would beat the famous *kirschwasser*.

Further on was a row of pineapples, on which subject Barbosa's easy, illuminating explanations had cleared up a host of doubts for her. How well she remembered the description which he had given her: *Bromelia ananas*, of the Bromeliaceae family; leaves in rosettes, hard, fragile, dagger-shaped, spiny, up to one metre long; flowers red or purple, emerging from a hard, blood red calyx, in petioles twenty to thirty centimetres long; fruit attractive, piniform, green, whitish, golden and red, consisting of a spiral series of berries fused and united to their neighbours, covered by scales ending in little scarlet leaves, the whole crowned by a spiky tuft. *Abacaxí, naná, macambira, onore, uaca, achupala, naná-iacua* were the names given in the South American continent to this delightful fruit, described by Ferdinand the Catholic of Spain in 1514 as the finest fruit in the world. Gonzalo Hernández, Lery, Benzoni, all described it in their works; Cristóvão Acosta gave it the name which it still bears. There are no less than eight varieties. It has penetrated Africa to the edge of the Congo, and Asia to the heart of China. In Pernambuco it is superb, but where it reaches the pitch of perfection in form, smell and taste, where it touches the divine, is in Pará.

Further on was a paw-paw...

Lenita shook her head, interrupting the flow of her ideas in desperation; Barbosa's teachings, his erudition, which she was reproducing, only intensified the pain of missing him.

She could not believe that he was absent: he was there, he must be there in the Colonel's saloon, mending a broken electrical apparatus; or on the veranda, looking up a Greek or Sanskrit root in a huge dictionary. Yes, he must be inside, at one of his usual tasks. Perhaps he needed her help...

And she ran in. Before she reached the door, she stopped. Madness — Barbosa was far away. He had gone, she had seen him go.

By now he would have gone about two leagues; six hundred and fifty chains; thirteen thousand, two hundred metres. Every minute took him one hundred and ten metres further from her. The next day, at exactly ten minutes past six in the evening, he should be, he would be, in Santos, forty-five leagues away, three hundred kilometres, three hundred thousand metres!

She went miserably to her room, lunched poorly and dined worse.

In the evening, as the setting sun flooded the landscape with torrents of soft, yellow light the colour of old gold, drawing out to gigantic length the shadows of animals, trees, houses and mountains, Lenita went out to sit under a thick cluster of brambles perched on an outcrop above the stream. Her chest felt constricted and her breathing was short and forced.

Hidden by the interwoven foliage, she overlooked a vast expanse of ground, as a visual radius drawn from her eye traced the arc of a circle. The scattered shapes of the big, very black cows with their white markings stood out strongly against the velvety green of the pasture.

A red Andalusian bull was lowing and pawing the ground in the distance. A flock of dark sheep, with very black faces and legs, was grazing nervously in ceaseless movement, nibbling the grass here and there. Almost at her feet, at the base of the outcrop with its brambles, the stream spread into a smooth rapid over its bed of little white pebbles. A thin clump of scrub ran away from the stream bank and petered out after a short distance.

Lenita gazed absently out at the wide scene, distracted, lost in herself, staring with unseeing eyes. A fierce lowing close at hand brought her back to the present.

The bull had approached a large cow, whose calf, already weaned, was grazing some way off, having almost forgotten the teat.

He arrived sniffing the air anxiously, smelt the cow's muzzle, smelt her all over. He raised his head, snorting loudly, as his lip curled back sensuously to expose his toothless upper gum. He gave a strangled bellow.

This was the sound Lenita had heard.

The bull licked the cow's vulva with his rough, slimy tongue; then, panting, his bloodshot eyes bulging, eager yet fearful in his erotic fury, he raised his forelegs and mounted the cow, covering her, his head hanging down to the left, flattening the tufted hair of his chest against her back.

The cow opened her hind legs slightly, arched her back; the skin on her flanks wrinkled as she received the fecundation. The act was consummated in one swift, sure, red thrust.

It was the first time that Lenita had witnessed large animals engaged in the physiological act by which life is reproduced.

Her cultivated spirit, far from judging it unclean or immoral, as hypocritical society is pleased to represent it, found it lofty and noble in its delightful simplicity.

A soft, languid whistling which drifted up from the stream made her turn her head. She looked and saw Rufina, a new black girl with firm, proud breasts and very white teeth.

She was splashing in the smooth water of the rapids, laughing with her head high, holding her skirts right up so that her pubis showed, and the matt, purplish black of her thick, muscular thighs.

Still whistling, she went up to the head of the rapids where the stream was a little deeper, raised her skirts still higher. Bundling up her clothing, she stooped and submerged her buttocks in the murmuring waters, and with both hands proceeded to carry out a thorough ablution, at once tonic and exciting.

Then, with the water still running in shining rivulets down the dark, dusky skin, she went into the scrub.

Her languid whistling could still be heard.

Before long it was answered by another whistle.

Running down a trail from the opposite slope came a strapping young negro. He swiftly crossed the rapids and disappeared in turn into the scrub.

The whistling ceased.

Lenita heard the confused, intermittent murmuring of voices, saw branches shaking; between the forks of two trunks, between the interweaving twigs, she half-glimpsed a sort of brief struggle, followed by a dull thud, the heavy sound of two bodies falling together to the sandy floor of the thicket.

Lenita understood rather than saw. Here was reproduced the event of just a few moments before, but at a more elevated level. The instinctive, brutal, fierce, instantaneous coupling of the beasts was succeeded by the conscious, voluptuous, loving, slow human coitus.

Shaken to the core of her being, her nervous irritation heightened by these scenes of crude nature, tortured by the *flesh*, gnawed by an insane desire for complete sensations as yet unknown, but guessed at, Lenita tottered weakly back to her room.

The Colonel had had a bad night with an attack of rheumatism, and had spent all day in bed.

Lenita went to see him, but did not stay long before she went back to shut herself in her room.

Chapter 10

Night had fallen.

There was no moon, but the night was bright. The stars were spread improbably thickly against the transparent tropical sky, like handfuls of luminous flour on a black cloth.

The yard in front of the slaves' quarters had been swept and a fire was crackling cheerfully, the glow from its heart and the constantly changing, flickering tongues of flame dispelling the darkness.

The slaves had finished weeding the canes that day and the Colonel had given them the rest of the day off, and had ordered the administrator to hand out a generous ration of cane spirit.

They were dancing to the sound of crude instruments — two *atabaques* and several *adufes*.[30]

Squatting with the *atabaques* gripped between their knees, coiled, hunched over the instruments, two robust old Africans beat on the taut skins with both hands to sound out a turbulent, nervous, wild, impetuous rhythm.

Men and women formed a wide circle, moving and clapping rhythmically, a few beating *adufes*. In the centre, a dancer leapt and spun, squatted and rose, his arms and neck writhing, swinging his hips and beating his feet in an indescribable frenzy, with a prodigality of movement, a nervous and muscular exertion which would have exhausted a white man in less than five minutes.

And he sang:

> *Serena pomba, serena;*
> *Não cansa de serená!*
> *O sereno desta pomba*
> *Lumeia que nem metá!*
> *Eh! pomba! Eh!*[31]

And the crowd repeated in chorus:

> *Eh! pomba! Eh!*

The singer's fresh, modulated voice, with its dark, rounded tone, held an infinite sweetness, an inexpressible charm.

---

[30] *Atabaque* a small drum. *Adufe* square tambourine.
[31] Let fall your dew, pomba [both a dove and an African spirit], let it fall;
let fall your dew tirelessly!
The dew of this pomba
Shines like metal!
Eh! pomba! Eh!

If one closed one's eyes, one would never believe that such pure sounds emanated from the throat of a dirty, ill-formed, stinking, revolting black…

The response of the chorus, a melopoeia lacking in harmony but cadenced in intervals of sweet, gentle sadness, echoed through the trees in the silence of the night with a strange, melancholy grandeur.

The words meant nothing, the melody, the singing was all.

And the *atabaques* beat, the *adufes* rattled furiously.

The dancer, still singing, still in his stupendous, manic choreography, went round the circle without pausing to draw breath, without any sign of tiredness. Not a drop of sweat gleamed on his matt head.

Suddenly, seeing a flaming brand in the hand of a comrade, he seized it and began to draw capricious figures in the air, circles, ellipses, figures-of-eight. He beat it on the ground, scattering thousands of sparks around the circle… The excitement rose to delirium.

The dancer threw down the brand, hurled it away with all his strength. Then his movements slowed, moderated slightly. He stopped before one of the men in the ring, swaying and gesturing, as if provoking him to come out into the circle.

The other accepted the challenge and stepped out towards him, dancing and swaying also.

Eh! pomba! Eh! moaned the chorus.

The dancers, two of them now, began to turn around one another, attacking, pursuing, fleeing, like two amorous butterflies. They withdrew, then advanced face to face, slowly, measuring one another up. Their arms hanging, their heads back, their stomachs protruding, their legs curved, they smacked their navels together in a resonant, artistic clash which reverberated into the distance.

Eh! pomba! Eh! the chorus moaned on.

The first dancer dived into the crowd, broke the circle and joined his companions, leaving his successor to continue the performance alone with the same vigour.

Those who were not dancing, not taking part in the *samba*, elbowed one another in tight little knots; they watched in silence, absorbed and entranced.

A cloud of dust, reddish in the firelight, rose from the earth beaten by the many stamping feet.

The demijohn of cane spirit passed from hand to hand. There were no cups, everyone drank from the flagon.

Above the smell of beaten earth, of cane spirit, of chewed tobacco, arose a dominant smell of humanity, harsh and garlicky; a strong, indefinable, musky, African odour, which assailed the sense, pierced the nerves, befuddled the brain, suffocating and unbearable.

While the dancing continued in the yard, Joaquim Cambinda, an eighty-year-old slave who was past work, sat alone on a section of tree-trunk before a fire of *perova* wood in the old abandoned shed which had been given him to live in.

He was a horrible sight: bald, thick-lipped, with outsized jaws and yellowish, bloodshot whites to his eyes which stood out against his very black skin. He was hunched with age, and when he stood up, wrapped in his brown woollen blanket, and took a few slow, stumbling paces, he resembled a dark, cowardly, savage, repulsive hyena. His hands were like dried up talons; his nail-less toes curled back horribly on themselves.

The old shed formed a broad square of broken tiles and pitted earth floor. On one side was a bedstead of round wooden bars, with a woven mat, a shiny black pillow and a few filthy rags, where the old man slept. In the dark space under the bedstead gleamed whitely an old earthenware chamber-pot with a broken lip, its fetid, nauseating base dotted with an archipelago of uric incrustations. Beside the bed stood a deal crate, with a brand new, varnished lock shining against the worm-eaten, smoke-blackened wood. On the other side, opposite the bedstead, on a table with a broken leg, stood a very old oratory[32] with worn, rusty hinges; it had been gnawed by mice in places, and was liberally covered with candle-wax. On the walls hung little sacks with tied mouths, woven fish-traps, narrow-necked calabashes, ox-horns, ancient top hats, archaic cloaks with threefold lapels from the king's days.[33] All over the floor were pumpkins, ripe cucumbers, corn cobs, heads of farming tools, sections of tree-trunks, egg-shells, cabbage stalks and heaps of rubbish.

The door was shut but not locked. It opened and a young negro woman came in; she was small and thin, with sunken eyes and a feverish look. She was dressed in startling colours, a yellow skirt and a scarlet jacket. She received Cambinda's blessing and went and sat down silently beside the fire.

---

[32] A small shrine or prayer-altar for private use.
[33] i.e. the period when João VI of Portugal (initially as crown prince) established his court in Brazil to escape from the Napoleonic invasion, 1808–1821.

One by one, other men and women entered. They stepped inside, paid their respects to the old man, then sat in silence around the fire on tree-trunks — ten in all.

When they had reached that number, Joaquim Cambinda said: 'Shut de door!'

The woman who had entered first stood up, obeyed and returned to her place.

Silence reigned for long minutes.

Outside, the chorus could be heard echoing in the night: *Eh! pomba! Eh!*

Cambinda had lit a long-stemmed pipe and was smoking quietly, apparently unaware of those around him.

He remained absorbed for nearly half an hour, his eyes closed, meditating, nodding, puffing out smoke.

When his pipe was burnt out, he knocked it firmly and carefully to shake out the ash, blew through the stem and stood it against the wall. Slowly and unsteadily, he heaved his monstrous form upright, walked over to the oratory and opened its little doors wide; he took out two wax tapers on tin candle-sticks, struck a match and lit them to illuminate the interior of the niche, lined with foreign-made silver paper.

There were two divinities in this miserable, sordid household shrine: a crude plaster St Michael, clumsy, very ugly, liberally covered in fly-spots; and a fetish woven entirely of very fine threads of *embira*,[34] stinking, horrible, but remarkable for its anatomical detail, a stupendous work of patience.

The negroes all rose reverently.

'Jerome,' said Joaquim Cambinda, 'you t'ink good 'bout what you go fer do, boy?'

'I t'ink good, *mganga*'[35]

'So you want fer join de Brudderhood of Saint Michael an' All Souls?'

'Is so, *mganga*.'

It was a fine thing, Cambinda explained in his curious jargon, for a negro to belong to the Brotherhood of Saint Michael and All Souls, but it was also dangerous — if he did not have the courage he should not take the oath. The white man wanted to find out the secrets of

---

[34] Vegetable fibre from a plant of the Annonaceae family.
[35] African name for the lord of the weather, the rain-maker, and thus a term of respect.

the brothers of Saint Michael by force, and so he beat the black man; but the negro who revealed the secret of Saint Michael would die mysteriously. He made the neophyte kiss the feet of Saint Michael, the horns of the Satan on which he stood, the genitals of the fetish. He administered solemn oaths, threatening terrible punishments if they should be broken. He received payment — thirty thousand *reis*, in six 5,000 *real* notes which Jerome produced from his trouser pockets, tightly rolled in a dirty piece of cotton print. He went on to the indoctrination, initiating him in the terrible art of spells and countercharms, teaching him to kill and cure. He taught him that the seed of the *devil's trumpet (Datura stramonium)*, crushed and macerated in cane spirit, makes the victim blind, drives him mad and kills him within a few hours; that a bone taken from a corpse, after the flesh has rotted away, ground up and mixed with any sort of food, causes incurable *amarelão*;[36] that the green toad of the jungle, suffocated over a slow fire in a new saucepan with a new lid, produces a white foam as it dies, which, diluted with water, causes an inevitably fatal dropsy; that the leaves of the *jaborandi (Pilacarpus pinnatifolius)*, pounded down into a paste and applied under the armpits, cause perspiration and salivation, and cure various illnesses; that the guinea root *(Mappa graveolens)* and *nhandirova (Feuillea cordifolia)* are powerful countercharms against all kinds of spells.

He taught him also a mass of superstitions, some terrifying, others frankly ridiculous: that the dried hand of an infant which has died un-baptized is a precious talisman for good fortune in love; that a chip of stone stolen from a church altar casts a spell over the body, making it invulnerable to firearms and steel; that coffee strained with bathwater through the tail of a woman's blouse or the seat of a man's drawers, unwashed, captures friendship and calms an aggressive spirit; that a rope which has been used to hang a man brings luck in gambling; that a knot from the root of a rue bush, torn up on Good Friday, is a sovereign remedy against the evil eye and its effects; that to incapacitate a sorcerer, to draw his power, you must beat him with a stick of tobacco and break three fertile eggs over his head.

He went on to *cure* the neophyte, to *seal* his body, deadening it against corporal punishment: he ordered him to strip and go down on all fours like an animal. Murmuring disconnected words,

---

[36] Hookworm disease was endemic in Brazil at this time and its nature not generally understood in the countryside, thus its common name refers to the yellow colour assumed by its victims.

mumbo-jumbo phrases, he anointed him with a rancid ointment which he poured from a rusty tin, spattered him with water from a gourd which he took down from the wall. He explained that it was necessary to repeat this ceremony on the next six Fridays for the spell to be complete and his body fully insensible.

To give concrete proof of his power, to demonstrate the effectiveness of his sorcery, he called the thin black woman who had been the first to arrive. She approached him quickly and eagerly.

A strange scene occurred.

From his oratory Joaquim Cambinda took a long, sharp sailor's needle, and grasping the woman's left arm he pierced it through in several places: not a drop of blood appeared. The patient observed her arm curiously without giving the slightest sign of pain.

Cambinda put down the needle, drew back a little, and squatted down. He looked at her strangely, under lowered eyelids, his eye bright and stony as a reptile's.

The girl screamed violently and clawed at her chest.

'Me ches', me ches'! Me can't breathe!' she cried.

She fell like a log, her eyes bulging, her mouth twisted, her convulsed limbs contorted and frozen.

Her arms stretched out stiffly, with the wrists twisted outward; her fingers clenched, the nails almost digging into the palms of her hands. Her tongue stuck out, black, streaked here and there with slimy saliva.

She writhed and twitched on the ground, like a snake cut into pieces.

Suddenly she gave a guttural, raucous, strangled, inhuman bellow. She shuddered and arched backwards like a catapult under tension, then froze, motionless, hard, tensed in an impossible position, supported at three points: at one end the top of her head rested on the floor, at the other her feet stood flat on the ground and slightly apart.

Her fists remained clenched, her arms tense along her sides. The body was corpse-like in its rigidity — more: like metal or marble.

Joaquim Cambinda smiled a ghastly smile.

With an agility which belied his customary halting decrepitude, and of which none would have judged him capable, he leapt onto this extraordinary human bridge.

His eyes shining, like the reflection of the firelight on his bald, polished black scalp, his yellow teeth gleaming in his diabolically contorted face, he writhed and pulsed on the stomach, the belly, the pubis of his convulsed subject.

She did not rock or yield beneath the thrust of the monster's legs, or the force of his weight; she seemed to be made of stone, like the arch of a bridge.

Joaquim Cambinda got to the floor again and went to fetch a pickaxe haft from a corner with which he began to beat her breast and abdomen.

The blows rained down with a dull, muffled sound, as if they fell on a sackful of rags.

Suddenly the victim relaxed, recovering her vital flexibility, and fell heavily to the ground in a human attitude. Her face was covered with fat beads of sweat.

The onlookers were terrified.

The vile hierophant of these horrible mysteries had rapidly snuffed the candles and closed the oratory. He was once more sitting silently on his trunk, stirring the fire.

The girl had fallen into a deep sleep, her breathing loud and stertorous.

Outside, the *samba* continued to the sound of the thumping *atabaques* and the dull stamping of feet. The refrain re-echoed, sonorous, melancholy, plaintive:

Eh! pomba! Eh!

Chapter 11

It was many days since Barbosa's departure, and all he had written was a business letter to the Colonel, saying that he hoped to salvage thirty percent of the merchandise.

At first Lenita sent the boy into town every day to fetch the post. Long before he was due to return, she was at the door looking out for him. When his outline, dressed in white cotton and joggled by the trot of an old grey donkey, appeared at the top of the hill as a moving white blob against the dull yellow of the road, she would run to meet him at the gate in the fence.

With feverish hand she took the leather satchel containing the correspondence from him and opened it; when only the newspapers fell out, she asked nervously, tremulously, cherishing a last glimmer of hope: 'And the letters? Where are the letters?

Her disappointment, her anger even, to hear the boy reply in his slow, gentle, indifferent, sing-song voice 'No letters,' were indescribable.

She lost interest, no longer sent the boy to town to fetch the post, and when he brought her the papers of his own accord she would say curtly: 'Put them on the table there.'

One day, among the maze of tiny print of the *Jornal do Comércio*, her eye lit on a bulky, swollen envelope. The blood rushed to her heart when she recognized Barbosa's handwriting on the smooth official paper of the envelope:

> To:
> Miss Helena Matoso.
> Vila de ***, Province of S.Paulo.

She seized it violently from the boy's hands, dropping the newspapers, which she did not trouble to pick up. She went to her room, clutching the envelope to her breast.

She locked the door from the inside and half-closed the shutters, leaving only a crack to let in enough light to read by. She did not want to be seen, or interrupted by anyone.

Trembling, her hands tingling, she impatiently, almost brutally, tore open the envelope.

The letter consisted of a great number of sheets of very fine paper, *pelure d'oignon*,[37] covered on both sides with copperplate handwriting and all efficiently numbered.

Lenita read:

---
[37] Onion-skin

Júlio Ribeiro

Santos, 22 January 1887.

Esteemed Companion of my studies,

Here I am for the first time in my life in the seaport of our province, in Santos, a hot, humid, suffocating place, preferred by Martim Afonso to the enchanting surroundings of Guanabara Bay.[38] The reverends Kidder and Fletcher, in the book which they published on Brazil, beat their brains to discover the reason for his preference, and came up with... nothing. I am in the same state. Really, why would Martim Afonso have preferred this to Rio de Janeiro, when everything would indicate that the contrary was the obvious choice? What intuition, what stroke of genius, what miraculous insight revealed to the Portuguese colonist the immense superiority of this area of São Vicente, with its reddish-black soil and its unrivalled climate for farming, over the arid, drought-stricken, brick-red soil of the coastal strip? The fact is that for no apparent reason, with no acceptable data, he acted on a preference, and this preference gave rise to the first province of Brazil, and perhaps the first of the world's small, free states.

I find myself cornered; what I want is to describe the climate of this sector of the coast, to find a comparison.

People talk of Senegal. Senegal is hotter, it is true, but not so suffocating. You may breathe fire there — but you can breathe. Here there is nothing to breathe, not even fire. The air is heavy and oily; it seems to be lacking an element, at least when the famous wind which the locals call the Northwester is not blowing. When it is, when this African simoon, this accursed vendaval *fills the air, Santos is an inferno in miniature. Imagine a typhoon in an oven!*

The days are horrible. If it does not rain, which is rare, the sun burns and sears the earth, to the point where you could fry an egg on the cobblestones of the street. But even worse than the days are the nights. The atmosphere is still, lifeless. You look at the flames of the ships' lights — motionless; the tops of the trees — motionless; the palm-leaves — motionless. The people suffocating in the dead, un-breathable air look like the mammoths found whole in the Siberian ice, or like those insects mummified thousands of years ago in the golden transparency of yellow amber. It is an affliction which drives you to desperation, weighs on

---

[38] The Portuguese explorer Martim Afonso de Sousa sailed into Guaranabara Bay on 1st January 1532 and gave it the name of Rio de Janeiro. However, the first settlement which he founded was at Santos, on the island of São Vicente.

your heart, gives you the urge to weep, reminding you of the horrors of Byron's 'Darkness'.

Life here is a negation of physiology, a true miracle. Complete haematosis never occurs, digestion is laborious in the extreme, people sweat as if they were in the second degree of pulmonary phthisis, or convalescing from recurrent fevers. For myself, if I were condemned to exile in Santos, not even for life but for a year or two, I would kill myself.

But what fish! What splendid seafood! The yellow jack are delicious, the groupers divine! In France I ate oysters from Cancale, Merennes and Ostende; I ate the Mediterranean pink oysters and the Corsican laminated variety. None of them can compare with the Santos oyster. Tender, delicate, flavoursome, it is that pale shade of green so appreciated by fine gourmets: Moquim Tandon, Valenciennes, Bory de St. Vincent, Gaillon, Priestley, Berthelot invented a thousand cerebral theories to explain it, and yet it is no more than the symptom of an indisposition, caused by a morbid state, an anasarca of the mollusc.

If the land and the climate in Santos are detestable, the fish is wonderful, and the people equally superior. Negative factors yielding excellent results; a truth which may be paradoxical but is absolute and undeniable.

The people of Santos are polite, affable, obliging and frank; the wealth which the city's trade earns them makes them generous to the point of prodigality. They are bold and energetic, the only people in this placid province whom I judge capable of revolution. Not long ago there was a problem with the water supply and they showed what they were made of...

I derive immense pleasure from both the fish and the people in Santos.

Now, a little study, so as not to lose the habit, to return to our hobby, our fad.

The coast of Brazil, as the Comte de Lahure so rightly observes in his work on the country, has a remarkable distinctive feature which runs from the Island of Maranhão to Santa Catarina: it is lined throughout its length by two shallow ridges, two reefs, which follow it and form a sort of natural mole which protects it from the onslaught of the eternally beating waves of the South American Atlantic.

One of these reefs, the closer inshore, is like a rocky band which envelopes the coastline. In places it follows the ocean floor, in others it sticks up without reaching the surface of the water; elsewhere it just breaks the surface, and there are parts where it rises high above it.

It is the breaks in this band of rock which form all the inlets, all the bays, all the ports, all the openings of the Brazilian coast.

The second division, like a barbican of the first, lies at a distance of between eight and forty kilometres, of irregular depth but usually shallow.

The exposed points form islands, some of which are very high. The Queimadas, the Alcatrazes and the Monte de Trigo are salient points of the outer wall. The islands of Enguá-Guaçu or Santos, of Guaíbe or Santo Amaro, of Moela, and the enchanting islet of Palmas, are peaks of the inner reef.

And what are these two reefs, these two rocky bands, but the emergence, the first low indications, still marine, of the Serra do Mar, called here the Serra de Cubatão or Serra de Paranapiacaba. From its roots in the depths of the sea, the range rises, emerges, soars up vertically; the backdrop of its towering ridges, glimpsed among the clouds, close the horizon and abut the sky like the walls and barbicans of a titanic castle.

Just consider; let your reason reconstruct what man, in his brief span of life, cannot witness.

Long ago, the sea used to wash the feet of the mountains, and the onshore winds, channelled up the valleys, carved fearful chasms in the plateau over which the train now puffs.

The floods, the mountain torrents heavy with soil, rolling huge boulders in their struggle against the force of the curling bores driven in by the tides, deposited sediment and detritus around the rocky nuclei of Guaíbe and Monserrate. Over hundreds of thousands of years, the sea bed rose and emerged from the waves, to form the broad plains which now skirt the mountains. Originally soft mud, swamps and tidal marsh, little by little these plains were covered with green mangroves, siruvas and later stronger vegetation. Solid land formed, crossed by a multitude of estuaries.

The plains of Santos, like all the plains of the Brazilian coast, are a conquest of the mountains.

And this conquest continues, and will continue indefinitely, day and night, every hour, every moment. Slow, imperceptible, but interminable, unceasing — there is no truce in the struggle between sea and land.

The shores of the estuaries — here called rivers — become narrower and narrower as the bottom rises. Martim Afonso's fleet passed through *the Bertioga passage with ease. Until a short while ago, the coastal steamer Itambé used to pass through. Today, the little tug Porchat has difficulty in passing, turning is hazardous and on occasion she runs aground.*

In the city of Santos there is no sea in the strict sense of the word. There is a brackish estuary which is shrinking, getting shallower every day. It is useless to resist. The famous and much postponed quay, if it is ever built, will provide temporary relief: it will improve the port for a few years but in the end it will be useless. The land is winning and one day it will win for good; the past points to the future. In vain the ocean, repelled and beaten back at one point, concentrates its forces at another and attacks São Vicente. It gained an apparent victory, it is true, over Martim Afonso's old settlement, and it threatens the modern one. But the enemy, the mountain, is there to halt it, to block it, to repel it with avalanches of stones and banks of mud.

There are other examples of this in the recent geographical history of the Old World. Louis IX of France twice boarded ship for the crusades in Aigues-Mortes, in 1248 and 1269. Today, Aigues-Mortes lies six kilometres from the sea. The city of Adria on the Canal Bianco, a distributary of the Po, today is thirty kilometres from the Adriatic. Well, it used to stand beside the sea, and even gave it its name.

Given the following facts there is nothing surprising in the Northwester, or in the heat of Santos.

The south-easterly onshore wind is channelled between the Santo Amaro and Monserrate ranges, whirls around the plateau, reaches the coastal range where it is repelled, and bounces back — but not alone. It comes back mixed and mingled with the hot wind from the interior, the wind heated over the dark red soil of the west, heated on the vast Piratininga plateau. That is the famous, the feared, the execrated Northwester.

To this is added chemical heat, the heat produced by the fermentation of incalculable masses of organic detritus, over a huge plain surrounded, almost enclosed, by mountains. Consider that only a minute part of all this heat is absorbed by the mountain walls, which reflect it back and focus it on Santos. Remember, too, that the proximity of the sea always tends to raise atmospheric temperature, and it is no longer surprising that this is the fifth highest thermal peak in the world, and that the only places which exceed it for heat are Abyssinia, Calcutta, Jamaica and Senegal.

Santos is a curious city. It has a colour entirely its own.

The houses are almost all built of masonry, with the thresholds and door-frames of dressed granite.

The salt in the air, which comes from the sea, attacks, erodes and eats away the stone. There are no smooth surfaces to be seen, everything is rough, crumbling, half decomposed.

On many of the roofs, aerial vegetation thrives, gloriously strong and vigorous.

Seen from the sea or the estuary, the city is black — the English call it Black town.

The huge German transatlantic steamers, the strange, bulky Austrian freighters, the ugly, white-sided British and American barques, the thousand transports of every nation, enter the river, come alongside the quay, moor almost on shore, ground their keels among the black mud, strewn with oyster shells, bones, shards of pottery, jars, tins, and old pieces of iron, all the thousand bits of filth which form as it were the excrement of a town. They are linked to the shore by long planks, either smooth or ribbed with creepers.

The streets are swarming with people of all classes and colours, coming and going, meeting and bumping into one another, carrying consignment notes, invoices, bank drafts, bundles of treasury bills, flat tin boxes with samples of goods. Huge, four-wheeled articulated carts, drawn by powerful mules, transport the bulging, golden, jute sacks, dribbling coffee, from the railway station to the warehouses, and thence to the wharves and the loading point. Men of brute strength, mostly Portuguese, carry them aboard on their heads, one or even two at a time, sometimes trotting to the beat of a monotonous, rhythmic chant, as compelling as the sound of the trumpet.

In the broad paved expanses of the warehouses, men wielding shovels, polished and worn with use, toss the coffee into piles, singing as they work.

Indeed, they have a certain barbaric elegance, with an empty sack draped over their heads like an Arab head-cloth, perhaps due to some unconscious, atavistic memory.

On the shore, a few metres from the water's edge, there is a sort of cosmopolitan market. The magnificent fish of the lagoon and the open sea, glinting steely or silver or gold, are laid out in lines on solid marble counters: fat, blunt-nosed tainhas, *and* paratís *which look like miniature versions of these; brown, hunch-backed* corvinas; *lean, flat* galos; pargos de dentes *with round, fleshy lips; huge, golden, deep sea fish; delicate, squinting plaice; smooth, flat soles, looking like huge plaice; stumpy, reddish groupers with bulging eyes, concealing in their clumsy shape a world of gastronomic delights; white and silver pescadinhas, their sides striped with a thread of golden-green; smooth, ugly, slimy bugres;*[39] *purplish white shrimps with long curling fringes, laid out on osier lids; smooth-shelled, slow-moving crabs, their shells clicking loudly against one another; blue land crabs.*

Under the eaves around the houses, oranges, pineapples, melons, guavas, coconuts, bunches of bananas and a thousand types of fruit are piled beneath cloth awnings in irritating, discouraging abundance, with that nauseous smell of over-ripeness. Grain, pulses, vegetables, tubers, herbs, tomatoes, peppers; animals and fowls, both wild and domestic, sucking pigs, quatis,[40] *turkeys, toucans; shells, water snails, mats, ropes, articles of hardware, an infernal confusion of junk.*

At three o'clock, activity starts to dwindle. The population emigrates to São Vicente and Barra. In the afternoon the city is silent, deserted, dead. Every day there is a sharp, abrupt, depressing transition from agitation to stagnation.

I went up the Montserrate.

This is a hill a hundred and sixty-five metres high, almost sheer, crowned by a white church; the most picturesque and charming sight imaginable, at once simple and grandiose.

The path up is hazardous.

The view which opens as you climb is simply wonderful. The plain which stretches into the distance, levelled by natural forces, is carpeted with mangroves. The city, laid out in regular square blocks, lies around the feet of this mound, marked by the dark lines of the paved roads, and here and there a green patch of trees or a tall, slender coconut palm. In the background to left and right are the mountains of the mainland, whilst opposite are the steep hills of Santo Amaro. The anchorage, the Canehu basin and other reaches of the estuary look like sheets of polished steel, with splashes of other colours formed by the ugly pontoons and the ships. Canoes and tenders skim swiftly, like insects; here and there a sail forms a white speck on the dark, metallic surface of the water, while the sun pours its soft, golden light over the whole scene.

Streams creep through the lush green of the mangroves. One is visible for miles as it winds into the distance; it skirts the foot of a conical hill called Monte Cabrão, disappears from view, only to reappear far away,

---

[39] A sort of crayfish.
[40] A small carnivorous mammal, sometimes domesticated.

glinting in the sunlight, before it is hidden for good. This is the historic Bertioga Channel.

To the right, a huge expanse of blue, which seems to stretch from infinity, to be folded in from the horizon, advances heaving, until it reaches the shore, kisses the beach, dies in a verge of trembling, murmurous white foam. Hail, Ocean! Alma pater, *laboratory of terrestrial life, peopler of the planet!*

Ah, Lenita, just imagine! The ocean — power, assault; the earth — strength, resistance; the air — haematosis, life; the sun — warmth, light, fertility; all in constant abundance constructing, adorning the vast scene of the 'struggle for life', where every creature in creation competes, fights, hunts, kills, eats — the zoophyte, the mollusc, the entomozoary,[41] *the vertebrate!*

Here, on these heights, beneath the immensity of the heavens, overlooking the immensity of the waters, one is filled with pride at the greatness of the talking anthropoid, who rips the sponge from the abyss, who paralyses the incalculable strength of the cetacean, who strikes down the swallow gliding through the void, who masters the ocean, who enslaves the lightning, who tears the veils of space, who exposes the mysteries of the infinite.

How I wish you were here beside me! How I wish I could see the fixed concentration in your eye, read in your pale face the deep impression that a banquet such as this would produce on a spirit such as yours!

....

Paulo minora cantamus[42]; *now* terre à terre.

This letter is going somewhat against the grain of the laws of chronology. I have inverted the order of events; I started at the end, talking of Santos, without mentioning the journey.

Now I will make good the fault with an amende honorable.

As far as the capital[43] *I saw nothing new. For many years I have known the railway line and all the different tracks linking the capital to the interior of the province. I have studied them closely and with a personal interest, as I hold shares in the Eastern Railway, incorrectly known as the Northern Railway.*

---

[41] This word, to describe insect life-forms, appears to have disappeared from use in English as in Portuguese.
[42] 'Let us sing of less lofty matters.' An intentional misquotation from Virgil (Eclogues IV, 1). *Terre-à-terre:* French — 'Down to earth'.
[43] São Paulo was capital of the province — the capital of Brazil was Rio de Janeiro

But from the capital to Santos I rolled into the unknown, finding new matter for study.

The famous plains of Piratininga form a plateau which undulates gently in rounded hummocks, framed on the right by the distant tops of the Serra do Cubatão and on the left by the bluish vistas of the Cantareira and the green peaks of Jaraguá.

Just north of the city, the deep, black, taciturn Tietê rolls from east to west, forming an immense, very wide valley.

The present-day conformation of this valley, the peat bogs of which it is largely composed, the flooding which occurs annually, all attest that it was once a vast, winding lake, dotted with islands, a fresh-water sea, stretching perhaps as far as Mogi das Cruzes.

The Cantareira mountains and the northern slope of the Serra do Cubatão fought an alluvial war against this fresh-water Mediterranean, conquered and filled it. The Tietê valley is the result of their victory. The year-round streams united and joined forces, dug out beds and formed the rivers which today cut across the plain.

I glimpsed the hall which is being built to commemorate independence, or rather to commemorate — why not admit it? — to commemorate the functional disorder which led Dom Pedro de Bragança to dismount there at four o'clock in the afternoon on 7th September 1822.[44]

In these parts you do not find the magnificent flora of our western countryside, the perovas, *the enormous* batalhas, *the jequitibás five metres in diameter: the boscage is fragile, low, almost dwarf. It is not dense and continuous, but forms clumps, spinneys, thickets, islands of greenery in the brownish yellow of the endless landscape.*

This region is considered to have poor, sterile soil: nothing is more unjust. It is true that coffee does not grow here, that the sugar cane is smaller than in Capivari or even in Santos, that the cotton does not compare with that in Sorocaba; but for God's sake, wealth is more than just coffee, sugar and cotton!

Vines grow at a surprising rate: with intelligent cultivation and early pruning they can fruit in early December, avoiding the January

---

[44] C.f. note 32. When King João returned to Portugal, his son Pedro remained in Brazil, where he sided with the nationalists and declared independence, subsequently being crowned Emperor. The official story is that he made his historic declaration — 'Independence or death!' — while travelling between Santos and São Paulo, on being handed a letter from his father ordering him back to Portugal. A more prosaic version has him dismounting under the effects of a bout of diarrhoea (Ribeiro's 'functional disorder'), upon which mutinous troops seized their opportunity and obliged him at gunpoint to break with the colonial power.

rains which make the grapes watery and produce rot in the bunches. In São Caetano, in land that used to be waste and considered useless, there are beautiful vines planted by the Italians. The symmetrical rows are a joy to see; the idea of immense, universal prosperity in the near future for every corner of our province — I was going to write 'state' — rejoices the heart.

The vegetables are enormous. The other day I saw a cabbage from São Paulo which was a monster: its leaves were fifty centimetres in diameter at their narrowest, the stalk measured much more than two metres.

And why should wheat not be grown here? It used to be grown successfully — a lot of bread from locally grown wheat was consumed in São Paulo. Everyone knows what scientific agriculture has done for the infertile Landes of Gascony. Well, the plains of Piratininga cannot be compared with the Landes: they are infinitely richer.

And stock-raising? What immense riches can be earned spontaneously.

From São Bernardo onwards the appearance of the plateau changes. The clumps and thickets give way to a huge, continuous, green-black forest. Here and there, on the hump of a hill or the crest of a mound, the line of a road snakes like a scarlet furrow. As the land rises, grasses appear, clumps of low plants with dark leaves and huge, purple flowers.

On either side of the train, dark, compact shadows pass fleetingly, cast by the first hills of the mountain range. Here and there bare granite appears, washed by streams, shattered by miners' drills or scarred by the sledgehammers of the rock-breaker.

On every tree hang parasites, with scarlet flowers and shining leaves.

The engine, panting noisily on its break-neck way, dragging its tender and long tail of carriages, climbs triumphantly upwards, conquers the steep gradient and reaches the top, rolling victoriously onto the plain. The air is thinner and moister, the light brighter and fiercer.

To the left, as if suddenly emerging, mountains, ridges, peaks, cliffs, precipices, shattered fragments of range seem to rise abruptly.

To the right, forming an amphitheatre against the eroded back of a hill, a few miserable huts; on the level summit stands a little rustic church, graceless, badly built, with three windows and two mock towers, a white dot against the blue of the sky and the dark jungle.

This is the crest of the range.

To our front, not many yards off, a void opens up, falling away into a huge empty space, bounded by a far distant horizon; an ash-grey confusion of mountain and sky which takes you by surprise, overpowering the imagination.

This is the start of those inclined planes on which, by the action of fixed engines, the Society of modern São Paulo ascends and descends — passenger carriages and goods wagons.

After you reach the crest and start the descent, the scenery becomes grandiose, imposing.

On one side close at hand, almost within arm's reach, are immeasurable heights cut vertically, covered in lichens and mosses, blocking out the sky. Though great caverns carved into these rocks roll murmuring waterfalls, foaming white, now in hissing threads, now channelled into torrents, now broadening into blades.

On the other, in the distance, the extent of the range in all its vast wilderness.

Mountains which brush the sky are raised on mountains, of which the seats are other mountains. Some forming sheer walls, others with rounded heads, others again in perfectly regular pyramids, their enormous mass overwhelming and crushing the spirit. You would think that this was where the giants scaled the skies, that this was the battlefield where the tremendous fight took place in which the sons of heaven suffocated the violent revolt of the sons of earth with terrible blows, with arms of every kind, with thunderbolts, hurling entire mountains.

Round the foot of these huge bulks runs a deep, deep valley, ending in fearful rock-falls, dizzying abysses, murderous precipices.

Rain-soaked vegetation — impenetrable, densely woven, inextricable — covers and stifles the mountainsides. Here you do not see the bare peaks of the mountain ranges of the old world; everything is covered with a carpet of dull dark green. From a distance it looks like a mat of weeds, close-to it is composed of enormous trees.

The canaleira with its pale green leaves points bright, cheerful notes in the sombre greenery, the flowering ipê *makes raw yellow splashes. The striking star-shapes of the crowns of the palm trees, in monstrous, incredible, obscene abundance, stand out among the confused mass.*

In the distance, on the hazy blue crest of the highest ridge, a long streamer of dazzling white mist, like the veil of a colossal uranid, torn and frayed in the gentle violence of an amorous encounter.

Only a stone's throw away, slender trees display the smooth, fleshy petals of white and red flowers on the same branch. The delicate, pale embaúva *trunks, with their dark foliage and scarlet shoots, stand up proudly.*

The sun's rays strike multi-coloured scintillations from the leaves of the neighbouring trees, cast handfuls of diamonds into the waterfalls. From a distance the reflections are absorbed, invisible.

At the end of the fourth inclined plane, the highest, you can make out the Grota Funda viaduct, a victory of daring over vastness, of iron over space, of the brain over raw nature.

Imagine, Lenita, a deep gorge; more than a deep gorge, a huge chasm; more than a huge chasm, a fearful abyss, crossed from side to side by an apparently airy bridge resting on immensely tall columns, so fine, so slender, that from a distance they look like wires.

To contemplate this astonishing void from the centre of the bridge makes your ears hum, your head whirl; vertigo seizes you, and the yearning for annihilation, the foretaste of nirvana, the delirium of height; it is only by a supreme concentration of the will that a man resists involuntary suicide.

As you descend, nature alters; the air becomes thick, heavy, hot, charged with nitrogenous emanations; coastal vegetation starts to appear, the slopes are covered by huge banana plantations.

A stratum of rock makes an angle in the inclined plane at the base of the range. As you go over this hump, there is a change of scene as in a magical play. The landscape suddenly opens out wide. From between mountainous heights and buttresses, which rise on either side like titanic bastions, spreads a broad, flat, smooth, level, brownish plain as far as the eye can see. From two hummocks to the right, round, smooth, symmetrically paired, reminiscent of virginal breasts, extends a dark horizontal line, absolutely straight. It is the sea, the ocean that gives its name to the range — Paranapiacaba.

A sort of furrow stretches across the plain, cutting across shining surfaces of smooth water here and there; and along this furrow, like a clumsy glyptodont, enormous, harnessed, zig-zags a hunched object, speeding smoothly and vomiting smoke. The furrow is the railway line, the glyptodont is the locomotive.

Below, where the plain begins, you can make out a cluster of wagons, looking like a herd of hippopotami asleep in the sun.

When a man stops to contemplate from the heights the stepped ridges of the mountain ranges, the valley cut by gorges, the plain, the coast, the line of the sea merging into the sky; when he observes the enormous forces at work in the earth's core and crust, in the water which laps it, the air which presses down on it, the light which illuminates it, the life which gnaws at it; when he extends and generalises the picture to consider the whole planet; when from there he passes to the neighbouring planets, to the sun, centre of the system; when he concludes by irrefutable induction that this sun, this centre, is in turn a moon, a humble satellite of some monstrously gigantic star blazing in the vastness, unknown, unknowable for all time; when he thinks that even this star orbits around another, and that about another; when he reflects that all this is a minute scene of the drama of universal life, and that the terrible, incomprehensible theatre of this interminable evolution is an insignificant corner in the immensity of space, he feels himself to be a minimal particle, an atom; he is overwhelmed, crushed by infinity, and his only consolation is in the idea of non-existence, of annihilation.

. . . .
. . . .

The English railway line from Santos to Jundiaí is a grandiose monument to modern industry.

From Santos to São Paulo it runs a distance of 76 kilometres. All the engineering work for levelling is admirably done, perfect. The distance to the foot of the mountains is 21 kilometres: there are three bridges, one especially noteworthy over an arm of the sea known as Casqueiro. It is 152 metres long, with ten identical spans, resting on extremely strong piers.

It is eight kilometres from the foot of the mountains to the plateau. The rise is 793 metres, giving a gradient of almost exactly ten percent.

How do they master these defiles, these dizzying cliffs?

Very simply.

The climb is divided into four uniform planes of two kilometres each. The drive is powered using a system adopted in some English coal-mines. Very powerful, fixed engines reel in and out a strong cable of twisted steel wire. Attached to the two ends of this cable run two trains: one ascending and the other descending. The needle of an odometer marks with mathematical precision the location of each train on the plane, and the moment when they cross. Operation can be stopped almost instantaneously by an extraordinarily strong brake, while an electrical apparatus provides immediate communication between the trains and their respective fixed engines. The cable, which is cooled by a jet of water at its exit, runs on vertiginously spinning pulley wheels with a monotonous, metallic sound, sometimes loud, sometimes very soft.

The service is regular and so well-run that for long stretches there is only one set of rails serving for both the ascent and the descent. The line has been running for more than twenty-one years without a single accident so far. Amazing, isn't it?

In each of the four stations with the fixed engines there are five boilers to generate steam, of which three are always working. The big grooved wheels which engage and release the cable, the piston-rods of polished iron which turn them, the brass bearings, the eccentrics in which the iron turns in the brass with smooth friction, everything is bright, gleaming, oily; everything functions like a healthy organism. Enormous chimneys of rusticated masonry, visible from a distance, disgorge gouts of thick swirling smoke into the air.

Rock-slides are shored up with masonry; all the permanent streams as well as the storm waters are directed and channelled through wooden spouts into stone or tile gutters with interlocking joints. There are granite underground ducts, with iron gratings, reminiscent of the dungeons of feudal castles.

In the Santos range the works of man are in harmony with the earth on which they rest; the visionary energy of art proves itself worthy of the overpowering scale of nature.

The Grota Funda viaduct is nothing short of a wonder. Its overall length is 715 English feet, more or less 215 metres. It has ten spans of 66 feet and one of 45 between two stonework buttresses; it rests on trellised iron colonnades (treillages) and on a pier at the upper end. The tallest column, including the base, is 185 feet high, 56 or 57 metres. The gradient is the same as the general gradient of 10%, or a fraction less. This astonishing work was started on 2nd July 1863; the first iron pieces were laid in March 1865; on 2nd November of the same year, the first train crossed — 2nd November, the Day of the Dead:[45] *the English are not superstitious.*

This railway company is an exceptional business. The results were beyond the most exaggerated expectations of optimism. The Governor General guaranteed five percent on the capital employed in the construction and the Provincial Governor two. However it is a long

---

[45] As All Souls' Day is known in Brazil. Naturally Ribeiro takes this opportunity to criticise the superstition of his compatriots.

time since the company waived the guarantee, and it has paid out fabulous dividends.

The English make money hand over fist, the riches of Croesus; and they deserve it. The astonishing progress of São Paulo, the industrial initiative of the modern inhabitant of the city, the network of railways which is the basis of life, commerce, civilization — to Botucatú, to São Manuel, to Jaú, to Jaguera, we owe it all to the Saint Paul Rail Road, the Santos to Jundiaí Railway.

Rule Britannia, Hurrah for the English! since our government is no good for anything.

This letter is getting long: it is time to put an end to it.

I have extended myself because when I write to you I imagine you at my side, and I want to draw out my illusion *as long as possible...*

I am old, and every old man is more or less authoritarian and pedantic. And you, Lenita, were kind enough to condescend to my advanced age; you listened to me, hung on my words, led me on to talk... So you must put up with the 'annoyance', with the 'choler', to use the classic term; the fault is yours.

I do not feel nostalgic for our shared life, our talks at home — the expression nostalgia contains too much poetry and not enough realism. What I feel is need; hunger and thirst for the company of someone who understands me, who makes me think... your company. Imagine — I spend the whole blessed day and half the night talking of nothing but coffee; but coffee from a commercial point of view, in shipments, in bags, in discounts... And I would be in a poor way if I did not: here, anyone who keeps off the subject, who does not talk coffee business, is taken for a fool.

I must explain something before I close. I have described in detail, perhaps too much detail, the mountains, the inclined planes, the works of art of the English company. How the devil could I have observed so much, grasped so many figures? In a rapid, dizzying descent in the train? Impossible! Inspiration, communication with spirits? Not at all. I must confess modestly that my sources are human: infused knowledge was the privilege of the apostles, of St Thomas, of Ventura de Raulica, and even today of Abbot Moigno and the Emperor of Brazil. These holy persons will not sue me for infringing their rights. Nor can I even boast of simple mental suggestion, of mere hypnotic teaching. I move in less elevated spheres, and learn what I know in a ruder fashion. One day having nothing to do I went to the top of the mountain and walked down, looking, observing and studying. There is nothing more to it.

I look forward to the day, I hope very soon, when I shall greet you with a firm, energetic, English hand-shake.

Manuel Barbosa...

Lenita read the letter impatiently: the details, the exact figures, Barbosa's scientific assessments of Santos and the mountains irritated her: she skipped over it all rapidly and nervously, without attention, as if skipping through a catalogue. She sought out any intimate reference to Barbosa himself, anything revealing which might betray the state of his affections.

She lingered over the final passages: she felt a lively, indescribable pleasure on reading that Barbosa imagined her at his side, and that the illusion gave him pleasure. She read the phrases syllable by syllable, almost letter by letter, her left eye closed, with absolute concentration. She was immensely pleased by the abrupt ending of the letter.

The erotic swoon which she had experienced in Barbosa's room served to confirm what she suspected: she recognized that she was profoundly, madly in love with this man.

Faced with this brutal fact, the pungent pleasure of the revelation of her flesh, her pride had revolted and she had taken refuge in a final effort at resistance, avoiding Barbosa on the eve of his departure.

But her insomnia each night, the huge vacuum left by Barbosa's absence, the fateful need, which she recognized in herself, of his presence to go on living, the pangs of desire, the victory of this new affection over the profound love which she had devoted to her father, Lopes Matoso; all this had convinced her that there was no turning back, that resistance was impossible.

With the swift decisiveness of a resolute spirit she accepted the yoke, submitted to her passion, admitted defeat.

That was the most difficult part.

In bowing she was ashamed of herself; once she became conscious of having bowed, she cared little that the whole world should see it.

In love but unconquered, she would struggle, would defend herself to the death against her desire, even in a bedroom, a place secret from all eyes; having yielded, defeated before her own intimate judgement, she cared not a fig for scandal, scorned public opinion, was capable of submitting to her conqueror in public, in an open square, like the prostitutes in Hyde Park.

She had confessed to herself that she loved Barbosa; she was capable of confessing as much to him, of proclaiming it to the whole world.

And she became indignant, blamed him for his timidity, wanted him to guess, to return her love, to feel the same for her as she felt for him, to confess in his turn that he was her slave, her captive. For her, Lenita, to love a man and not see that man surrendered, annihilated, devoted at her feet?! Impossible!

She re-read the letter, studying it attentively and thoughtfully. Barbosa's original assessments, his profoundly individual way of seeing things, the enthusiasm to communicate which sometimes carried him away, all this brought him to life, made him present in the letter, to the point where Lenita seemed to sense him beside her, to hear his voice, to feel his breath.

His theories on the formation of the Santos plateau or the filling of the Tietê valley made her think back and remember. She had once been in São Vicente to bathe. She knew Santos and the mountains. The facts given by Barbosa were exact, the explanations which he offered were plausible.

Lenita was filled with growing admiration for the flexibility of his talent, which extended to every subject, showed judgement in every field, made correct assessments on any head.

Her admiration for Barbosa's powerful intellectual faculties evolved passively, naturally, into an admiration for his body, a physical desire which drove her wild, demented.

Now she understood perfectly the story of Potiphar's wife in the Bible. The assured judgement which Joseph, the Hebrew slave, displayed, his exceptional administrative ability, his intransigence, his energy, his modesty, caught the eye of the Egyptian beauty. She was captivated by the sight of his slim, supple, youthful form; with ardent frankness she provoked and assailed him.

Lenita was roused to sympathy for this woman, stigmatized through the ages, but who was so adorably human, fleshly, real. She understood her, justified her, saw in her a reflection of herself.

Chapter 12

The black foreman had come to tell Lenita that birds were gathering in large numbers on a fruit tree in the jungle.

She ordered a trail to be cut from the track to the tree, had her Galand shotgun cleaned, loaded two hundred cartridges, and the following day before dawn set out with her maid to lie in wait.

Not much dew had fallen, and it was still very dark.

The trail, covered with a velvety layer of fine, yellowish sand, was wet from the thick mist which lay draped over the earth. The jungle formed a compact black mass. In the pastures, the occasional lone tree loomed out of the mist like a gigantic spectre.

There was a dry, sharp, healthy chill to the air. Suddenly, Lenita saw something rolling in the damp sand of the path twenty metres ahead. She stopped abruptly, brought the gun to her cheek almost without aiming, and fired.

'What was it, Miss Lenita?' asked the mulatto girl.

'Go and see — it's there, still moving,' returned the young lady, breaking the gun and loading a new cartridge.

And indeed an animal was writhing convulsively, scratching at the sand and scattering it broadcast.

The girl approached nervously, her body arched back, her neck outstretched.

'It's a *candimba*!' she cried jubilantly; and bending down she gathered up a superb hare which, although wounded in the head, was still alive.

Lenita took the soft animal from her hands and examined it with the voluptuous, triumphant pride of the impassioned hunter. She stroked the silky fur, smoothing it against her cheek, then put it in a net bag which she handed carefully to the black girl.

It was getting light, the veil of mist was thinning. The uncertain black of the forest was turning to green. The festive *taquara* bushes became visible, the bright crests of the palms, the opulent crowns of the *paineiras* literally coated with a pink covering of early flowers.

The sharp perfumes of fragrant orchids, freshened by the morning breeze, delighted the sense of smell, neither irritating nor dulling the nerves.

Birdsong started to be heard, and the humming of insects, in a festive hymn, a salute to the dawn.

Lenita and the servant girl penetrated into the jungle — here all was inky gloom. The fine dew which had fallen during the night had condensed on the leaves and dripped with a soft, dull sound onto the carpet of dead foliage which covered the ground.

Their lungs drew deeply of the pure oxygen expired by the vegetation around them.

The two women walked down the broad track together until they came to a tall *peroveira*, from the foot of which the trail plunged into the jungle to the left. They followed the trace until they stood below a slender *canaleira* in early fruit.

Silence reigned, broken only by the occasional soft dripping of the fine dew.

Lenita told the servant girl to move away a little and sit down, hidden behind some other tree. She looked up.

The foliage of the *canaleira* was outlined vaguely against the dark sky. Suddenly it became clearer, splotched with yellow, as if painted with a spray of liquid gold: the kiss of the first rays of sun from the rising dawn.

The treetops were already full of light and life; below all was still dark and mysterious.

A dark shadow flashed across the sky — a *jacuguaçu*. It alighted, swaying, on one of the lower branches. As it settled it slowly folded its raised wings, still using them to balance, and closed the beautiful fan of its long tail, stretching out its neck to peer cautiously to left and right.

After a few moments of observation, it climbed up the branch, navigated by hops through the foliage, then vanished and reappeared on the highest point of the crown, displaying its red wattle picked out by the sunlight.

Pale with excitement, her breast heaving, her muscles slack and her legs weak, Lenita watched the wonderfully elegant bird in ecstatic contemplation.

With an effort she raised the gun, bringing it up slowly and gently to sight.

She could not bring herself to fire. She lowered the gun and fell into renewed contemplation of the *alector*.

Suddenly her shining black eyes flashed, her features tensed, the white teeth bit the red nether lip; with cold determination she raised the gun once more, aimed and squeezed the trigger to fire.

On receiving the shot, the *jacuguaçu* fell tumbling to the earth, landing with a dull thump.

Leaping like a cat, Lenita grasped it, trembling with ferocious delight. She raised it to her face and blew apart the speckled feathers of its breast in order to inspect the wounds. With indescribable voluptuousness she felt the wetness of the warm blood running over her fingers.

The gun was still unloaded when she heard a strong, intermittent beating of wings.

She looked up.

On the same branch where she had shot down the *jacu*, the multi-coloured reflections of the graceful breast of a *pomba legítima* were shining in the sunlight.

Lenita quickly broke the shotgun, loaded, swung it up and fired, and the fresh victim fell wounded, thrashing desperately in its death-throes.

The servant girl, her eyes shining, her face glowing with enthusiasm, ran up to put the dead birds into a bag.

'A pigeon and a *jacu*, Miss Lenita!' she exclaimed jubilantly.

'Quiet!'

A toucan had just alighted on the fatal branch, turning its big, spongy bill this way and that. A marvellous effect was created by the contrast of the black feathers on its back with the proud orange of its throat and the vivid red of its breast: seeing it there showing off the splendour of its markings in the burning tropical sun you would have called it a beast of fantasy, a living, breathing flower, flown in from some unknown region to land in the tree.

Lenita brought it down with one sure shot, and another after it, and another; and then *araçaris*, turkeys, parrots — it was sheer butchery, devastation.

The time was almost ten o'clock; the sun was high in the sky, pouring down torrents of light; the long leaves of the *caetê*, the cordate leaves of the *periparoba* languished under its fiery kiss. A few wisps of pure white cloud dotted the bright blue sky, and a solitary vulture, lost in the vastness, sounded a black note in this festival of cheerful colours.

The heat was intense.

'It's late — it must be past lunch-time,' said Lenita. 'Let's go, we can come back tomorrow.'

'What a bag, Miss Lenita! Nineteen big birds and a hare. You didn't miss a shot.'

'I never miss a shot,' replied the young lady fatuously.

'Then you are like me,' said a voice behind them. 'I never miss a shot either.'

It was Barbosa.

The gun fell from Lenita's hands. Her heart faltered, unable to pump the blood into the arteries; pale, with a mist before her eyes, she had to lean against the smooth trunk of the *caneleira* to save herself from falling in a faint.

'What's the matter, Miss; what is it Lenita?' Barbosa came up and supported her carefully.

'You gave me a fright…' she murmured, recovering with difficulty.

'Forgive me, I was rash. I was eager to see you, I wanted to give you a surprise… Can you forgive me?'

He took her cold hands and pressed them in his own.

'Forgive you? I am so grateful to you for giving me the pleasure of seeing you the sooner. How did you arrive at this time of day?'

'I came on horseback, to gain a few hours. I rode all night. When I reached Jundiaí yesterday I had missed the train. I should still be there waiting. I hadn't the patience.'

'You didn't write to say you were coming…'

'I finished my business unexpectedly the day before yesterday. The others were stubborn, they had locked themselves into their proposal. Suddenly, when I least expected it, they changed their minds, gave in and accepted my conditions; and that was that.'

'Satisfactory?'

'As satisfactory as could be hoped for.'

'My sincere congratulations.'

'Thank you. But what a slaughter — what a St Bartholomew's day![46] You've bagged a whole flock! Upon my word! *Araçaris*, toucans, pigeons, *sabiacis*, a *jacu* and a *serelepe*… no, it's not a *serelepe*, it's a *candimba*, a hare, a big one! Well, well — a regular Diana!'

And he began to examine the bag with the air of an enthusiastic amateur.

'Tell me,' Lenita asked 'what is the name of these green birds with a round bill?'

'They are called *sabiacis*.'

'In Brazil, are the Psittacidae represented only by *arás* and parrots?'

---

[46] A celebrated massacre of Protestants occurred in Paris on St Bartholomew's Day 1572.

'Yes, in São Paulo at least.'

'How many species of parrots do we have?'

'As far as I know, six: *tuins, periquitos, cuiús, sabiacis* — these here — *baitacas* and true parrots.'

'And *arás*?'

'Four: *tirivas, araguaris, maracanans* and *araras*.'

'Ten in all?'

'So far as I know; there may be more in the dry country.'

'There I go with my fad for science! Enough ornithology! You must be exhausted — and famished.'

'Not exhausted, no. I have a bit of an appetite.'

'Then let us go and have luncheon.'

'I must confess I would enjoy that.'

They went.

Lenita was immensely happy, grateful even, that Barbosa had surprised her in the jungle, and had not waited for her at the house. Her pride as a woman was flattered. What was more, Barbosa had forgotten, or pretended to forget, her just but unjustifiable ill-temper on the eve of his departure. She loved him, and was convinced that he returned her love.

As they walked up the trace, what a world, what an infinity of small pleasures! Here a fallen, rotting tree trunk to step over, there a thorny branch to avoid; a steep, slippery slope to climb. Barbosa helped her round these obstacles, took her shotgun, offered her his hand. She let him help her, accepting his assistance not because she flagged or stumbled, but to place him in the role of the strong man, the protector. She felt an ineffable pleasure in being a woman so that he could be a man. His gentle, masculine voice caressed her, stimulated her brain, enveloped her in an atmosphere of harmony and love.

Unconsciously, unaware of the distance, they arrived home.

The Colonel was waiting at the door for them.

'So you had no trouble finding Lenita,' he called. Then, seeing the bag: 'What have you got there my girl? Eeh! What slaughter! There can't be any birds left in the jungle! This girl...! You should have been born a man... Who knows, perhaps you really are?'

Lenita coloured up to the ears.

The Colonel appeared not to notice her discomfort.

'Come, let's go and have luncheon, Manduca must be ravenous. The crazy fellow rode all night. Come along!'

Luncheon was a pleasant meal, but ended on a disagreeable note. As they were having coffee, the obligatory conclusion of luncheon in rural São Paulo, a terrified old black woman came into the room.

'Come quick, Sir!' she said. 'Maria Bugra is dying.'

'Where is she? What's the matter with her?' asked the Colonel in surprise.

'I don't know what the matter is. She's outside in the hall. I had her brought up.'

The Colonel rose and went to see; he was upset and walked with difficulty. Barbosa and Lenita followed.

In the entrance hall, lying on a leather-covered litter and resting on a morocco leather pillow which had once been red, was quite a young Fula[47] girl.

Her face was swollen, her breathing laboured, and the sinews of her chest were taut; her eyes were bulging and the pupils were excessively dilated, to the point where the border of the iris had disappeared. From between her deformed, contracted lips ran threads of viscous, resistant, translucent saliva.

The Colonel approached the patient and took her pulse.

'What do you make of this, Manduca?'

Barbosa approached in turn and placed the back of his hand against the black woman's face to feel her temperature — the skin was cold. He felt her pulse and found it weak and very slow. He pinched her, and she appeared not to notice.

'How did this begin?' he asked the woman who had brought the news.

'Well, young Massah, Maria was in the store-room de-graining maize, quite untroubled. Suddenly she started to complain that she felt uneasy; she stood up, started reeling and screaming and talking nonsense. She butted things with her head, foamed at the mouth, tried to bite people — she seemed crazy. Then she fainted and fell down, as she is now, so I had her brought here and called the master.'

'Ah. How long ago was this?'

'Just now, Sir.'

'Did she eat or drink anything?'

'She had luncheon, must be a couple of hours ago.'

'Did she drink anything?'

'She had some coffee, half a mug.'

'Where did it come from?'

---

[47] A West African ethnic group

'From Father Joaquim's hut.'
'Joaquim Cambinda?'
'Yes Sir.'

Barbosa went to his room, returning in a moment with a little flask of liquid, clear as water. He asked for a spoon — one was brought. He called the sick woman by name, close to her ear.

'Maria!'

She did not reply.

'Maria!' he said again, louder.

The woman made an effort to rouse herself from her soporific state and tried to raise her head, but in vain; she fell back heavily on the pillow, uttering confused, semi-articulate sounds. From beneath her clothing issued the fetid smell of faecal material.

Barbosa, seeing that he could get nothing out of her, that her will was destroyed, passed the flask to the Colonel.

'I'm going to open her mouth with the spoon. You pour in the contents of this bottle.'

'All of it?'

'Yes. It's a strong emetic; we need to make her vomit.'

With some difficulty he introduced the end of the spoon between the patient's teeth, and used it to lever to open her jaws.

'Now, Father!'

The Colonel emptied the liquid from the flask into her mouth as his son held it open.

'Swallow!' cried Barbosa.

The woman made an effort, retched violently and the spoon flew out of her mouth; the rejected liquid fell on the litter and ran over the floorboards. She was unable to swallow.

'Shouldn't we call Doctor Guimarães?'

'It's useless, Father. There's nothing we can do in this case.'

'Even so …'

'Doctor Guimarães couldn't get here before this evening; she will be dead in an hour.'

'Listen, Manduca…'

'I know what this is, Father. There's nothing we can do.'

The Colonel returned sadly to the dining room, accompanied by Lenita and Barbosa.

They sat down dispiritedly beside one of the windows. The woman's illness had cast them into profound dejection, an apprehension of vague threats and unidentified dangers.

They exchanged glances, unwilling to risk a word.
Yet this reserve weighed on them, the silence was unbearable.
It was broken by Barbosa.
'Father, Maria Bugra is dying. Do you know what of?'
'I am afraid to think it.'
'I see that you understand me. She is dying of the same thing as several other slaves on the *fazenda*, she has been poisoned.'
'It is a possibility.'
'It is not a possibility. It is a certainty. Do you remember the death of Carlos? And Chico Carreiro? Antonio Mulato? Maria Baiana?'
'Perfectly!'
'Didn't they present the same symptoms as Maria Bugra?'
'By Jove! You're right, they did.'
'Temporary violent excitement, delirium, followed by almost complete paralysis; swollen face, bloodshot conjunctive ring, bulging eyes, dilation of the pupils, inability to swallow, slow pulse, chilling of the body, urinary and faecal incontinence.'
'Exactly.'
'Well all this, I am convinced, is the consequence of the ingestion of a terrible poison, which is unfortunately very common here, atropine.'
'Atropine, very common here?'
'Yes.'
'But does atropine not come from belladonna?'
'It *also* comes from belladonna.'
'And where can you find belladonna in Brazil? Only in a botanical garden!'
'Don't you know that plant, Father?' And Barbosa pointed to a huge expanse of land covered by small, dark shrubs with serrated leaves and white, trumpet-shaped flowers.'
'Of course,' the Colonel replied. 'That's devil's trumpet, or jimson weed; terribly poisonous, they say. But you spoke of atropine.'
'The scientific name of devil's trumpet is *Datura stramontium*: you can extract a highly poisonous alkaloid from it, called *daturine*. However, Ladenberg and Schmidt have shown recently that daturine is quite simply atropine, the same lethal atropine which is obtained from belladonna.'
'And it is your belief that...'
'That Maria Bugra is dying from poisoning with a concentrated extract of datura seeds, and thus with atropine.'

'And have you a suspicion as to who administered the poison?'
'Not a suspicion, a certainty.'
'Who do you think it was?'
'Joaquim Cambinda.'

The accusation was made precisely, formally, with conviction. The Colonel lowered his eyes. He thought Barbosa was right. The *fazenda* had lost a number of slaves who had died from a peculiar sickness, invariably with the same succession of symptoms. This had begun after the arrival of Joaquim Cambinda. He had received this slave, already too old to work, among a number inherited from an uncle. He had never demanded service of him, and had given him lodging at his own request in an abandoned store-room standing by itself at the end of the yard. Some years ago, a white foreman had died on the *fazenda*; his widow, the Colonel remembered well, had created a tremendous, infernal scandal, saying that her husband had been killed by witchcraft, and roundly accusing Joaquim Cambinda. The Colonel had not attached much importance to the accusation, but now it had reared its head once more in the mouth of his own son, an intelligent, educated, sensible man.

'What are your reasons for accusing the old black?' he asked, after a few minutes' meditation.

'They are many. Firstly, the indisputable facts of the poisonings, which only began ten years ago when Joaquim Cambinda came to the *fazenda*. I was not here, but information reached me which kept me abreast of events. Secondly his fame throughout the district as a master of witchcraft; several people of sound judgement have had their doubts about him. Then I myself came across him, only the other day, drying snake' heads, *cicuta* and guinea roots, and datura seeds. What is more, he was... displeased with Maria Bugra.'

And Barbosa emphasised these words, his eyes on Lenita.

'That's true enough, I know, I even had to take measures on that account. But these are no more than assumptions...'

'Which together lead to conviction.'

'We need to clear this up.'

'I think so too. We cannot allow such a serious affair to lead to a rebellion.'

Barbosa's predictions proved correct. Maria Bugra passed from her soporific state to a coma, and from coma to death.'

In the evening, as dusk fell, after roll-call, the Colonel sent for Joaquim Cambinda. The fearsome old negro appeared, dragging his feet and leaning on a stick, with the filthy, brown blanket which he always used trailing on the ground.

When he arrived he entered the ante-room, leaning his stick in a corner.

The body of Maria Bugra lay stiffly on the litter in the middle of the room, covered by a thin linen sheet which picked out her hard, angular form. Four wax candles combined with the last glow of the day to cast a lugubrious light over her.

Mingled with the sharp smell of rancid vinegar and the nauseous smell of burnt lavender, a fetid odour could be detected, a whiff of putrefying flesh, of decomposition.

Joaquim Cambinda entered and looked indifferently on the dead body, then addressed the Colonel, who, together with Barbosa, had been waiting for him.

'Christ and de saints bless Massah. Massah call ol' negro, ol' negro here,' he said in his horrible, barbarous, irreproducible jargon.

'Do you know who is lying there dead, Joaquim?'

'Yes, is Maria Bugra.'

'Do you know what she died of?'

'Of her complaints.'

'What complaints?'

'I don't know, I no doctor.'

'So you don't know, you're not a doctor. And you don't know what Maria Baiana died of either — or Antonio, or Carlos, or Chico Carreiro?'

'How I should know, Massah?'

'If you don't confess to all you've done, here and now, I'll send you straight away to be finished off with the *bacalhau*. You damned sorcerer!'

'Ah, Massah! Sorcerer? This old negro who'll soon be accounting to God for all de beans he ate?'

'Stop your lying prattle! Come, what did you use to kill Maria Bugra?'

'I didn't kill her with nothin', Massah. How I can confess you something I never done?'

'We'll soon see whether you did it or not. Pedro, João, come here, tie up this rascal!'

The negroes were gathered round the door in curiosity, those behind stretching their necks to see over the shoulders of those in front.

The two summoned by the Colonel pushed their way through their comrades into the ante-room.

'Bind this lying scoundrel and take him to the trunk shed. I'll be there shortly. Take the *bacalhau* and a calabash of strong brine.

'What massah go' do with me?' asked Joaquim Cambinda quickly.

'You'll see.'

'Massah, Joaquim Cambinda never felt the *bacalhau*...'

'Now you're going to. There's a first time for everything.'

A terrifying transformation took place in Joaquim Cambinda. He threw away his ragged blanket, straightened his hunched trunk, raised his head, clenched his fists and faced the Colonel. His eyes blazed, his lips were drawn back to reveal his teeth.

'Ah, you want to know, I'll tell you: it was me who killed Maria Bugra!'

'Why did you kill her?'

'Because she was eating up my money, and she was tricking me with the young blacks.'

'And the others? Carlos? Maria Baiana? Chico Carreiro? Antonio Mulato?'

'It was me who kill them all.'

'What for?'

'Maria Baiana for the same reason I killed Maria Bugra. The others, to hurt you.'

'To hurt me? Why? Aren't you as good as free? Do I require any service from you? Don't I give you shelter and food and clothing? Why do you want to hurt me?'

'Now I've started to talk, I'll finish. You are good to me, is true; but you're a white man, and black man's duty is to hurt white man all he can.'

'Killing five of my slaves!'

'Five! Just babies I've sent off seventeen! Never mind grown black men: Manuel Pedreiro, Tomaz, Simeão, Liberato, Gervásio, Chico Carapina, Big José, Little José, Quitéria, Jacinta, Margarida, what did they die of? I kill them all!'

A loud murmuring arose among the group of negroes. Shouts and curses were heard.

'Now you are lying again — Little José died of a snake-bite.'

'What snake! The snake that bit him had no poison. He died from the medicine I give him.'

'But all these poor devils were blacks like you. Why did you kill them?'

'To make you poor. I wanted to see you work with your own two hands.'

'And you never tried to kill me?'

'Kill, no. Jus' hurt.'

'So you always wanted to do something to me?'

'Want! I did so!'

'Did so? What did you do?'

'What your rheumatism then? Where did the palsy old mistress have come from?'

And the negro laughed fiercely.

The Colonel was thunderstruck.

'Take this serpent away,' roared Barbosa. 'Put him in the trunk, let me never set eyes on him again! He'll be taken to town tomorrow.'

The negroes seized Joaquim Cambinda, who offered no resistance. They surrounded him and jostled him out into the middle of the yard.

'So, you killed my father!' said one.

'My mother!' shouted another.

'My three pretty babes; their heads and stomachs started to swell one time, they turned yellow and died with their little legs thin like frog's leg!' wailed a woman; and snatching up a broken tile from the ground she began to beat the sorcerer in the face.

This acted as a signal.

All the negroes swarmed round Joaquim Cambinda, some punching him, others spitting on him or throwing sand in his eyes.

'Damn plague! Evil thing!'

'Sorcerer from hell!'

'Let's hang the devil, now!'

'Burning is better!'

'Burn him, burn him!'

In horrific confusion they dragged the unfortunate away.

Beside the store-room was a pile of dry *sapé* grass, and nearby the floor of an old cart, falling to pieces, half rotten, with a single wheel. In a moment they had tied the miserable old man to this cart, despite the desperate resistance which he now put up, kicking, flailing and biting.

They brought armfuls of *sapé* and stuffed it into the space under the cart.

'Kerosene!' called out a voice, 'Bring kerosene.'

A boy ran to the mill-house and came back with an almost full can.

One of the men took it and mounted the cart, and began to pour the oil over Joaquim Cambinda; the liquid ran in a thick, clear, transparent stream, with bluish tints. It splashed up off the old man's hairy chest and shining bald scalp, soaked into his filthy clothing, mingled with the sweat which started from him in fat drops. The wretch's bloodshot eyes revolved, his teeth ground, his breathing was laboured.

'Matches, matches! Who's got matches?' the man asked, once he had emptied the can, and Joaquim Cambinda was buried beneath a mound of *sapé*.

'Me!' the negress who had started the riot ran up and passed him a box of matches.

The man jumped off the cart, took the box, bent down and lit a match. He cupped his hand to protect the flame and touched it to the *sapé* close to the ground.

A plume of thick smoke rose, pale blue at the top, reddish near the base. The fire flared up in long, greedy flames, licking at the cart on all sides, seizing on the *sapé* piled over the negro's body. His oil-soaked clothes seemed suddenly to explode into flame. He let out a hoarse, suffocated bellow, writhing frantically...

The scene was hidden in a crackling whirl of smoke and flame.

Sparks drifted off, the wind carried the charred seed husks into the distance.

There was a nauseous, acrid smell of burning, of fried fat and roasted flesh.

Chapter 13

In 1887, life in the interior of São Paulo province was still completely feudal.

The provincial *fazenda* was in every way the equal of a self-governing statelet of the Middle Ages. The *fazendeiro* had a private prison, and enjoyed *legal jurisdiction*; he was indeed *lord and master*. In ruling his *subjects* he was guided by a single code — his sovereign will. He was indeed beyond the reach of justice; he was not subject to the written laws.

At every moment and in every respect he could count on the unfailing acquiescence of the authorities, and on the rare occasions when he appeared at the bar of a court for some especially egregious and outrageous abuse of power, he was invariably absolved.

His power was such that he would sometimes order the murder of free citizens in the city; he showed scant respect for the constitutionally appointed authorities, which he flouted in the full exercise of their duties, and yet... he was absolved.

To maintain the *fazendeiro* in the possession of his customary privileges, illegal and immoral judicial practices had become established. In Campinas, for example, any crime committed by a slave, under whatever circumstances, was systematically declassified. The sentence, when there was one, was the minimum; and it was often commuted to a whipping, after which the criminal was returned to his master for him to exact private vengeance.

News of this frightful occurrence, the horrific lynching of the sorcerer by the slaves of the *fazenda*, did not get out; or if it did, if any hint of it reached the ears of the town authorities, they made no move.

The Colonel, who was a good, compassionate man, was at first horrified by a deed which he could do nothing to prevent. But in the end he understood that it was no use crying over spilt milk, and even felt that the example would not do any harm. Barbosa, although he had spent a large part of his life in the *philanthropic* Isle of Albion, was a *fazendeiro*'s son, brought up as such: he was not much surprised at the event and indeed was satisfied with the solution which it had provided to a complicated and very serious case.

The melancholy, dispirited atmosphere invariably generated by tragic events dissipated little by little.

Life on the *fazenda* returned to normal, indeed, it seemed to have improved, to have become more comfortable. Joaquim Cambinda had inspired fear, none had dared say a word against him, and even now, apart from the small group of his adepts, he was generally hated. His death, like that of every tyrant, had been a cue for general rejoicing, allowing expanded lungs to drink long draughts of air. The invisible, terrifying danger which had hung constantly over them all had disappeared

A mass of birds of different species continued to frequent the fruit tree, together with *serelepes* and even *ouriços caixeiros*.[48]

Lenita continued with her morning *razzias*.[49] Now Barbosa accompanied her, leaving her all the pleasure of the hunt and keeping the work for himself. It was he who went to look for the dead birds, who pursued and captured those which fell wounded. Having found a game trail some distance from the *caneleira*, he chose what he thought was a suitable spot, made a fair-sized clearing and put down maize to attract the animals. On the third day he noted with indescribable pleasure that the game was coming and had been eating the maize. Before long he had to put down more, there was none left. He saw that it was time to build a hide, which he made square, big enough for two people. He covered it all round with *guarirova* palm, and inside he made a solid, relatively comfortable wooden seat. In the floor he stuck forked sticks on which to rest the guns, and he made peepholes through which to spy on the game. He took pleasure in anticipating the delightful surprise which he would give Lenita, the ecstatic excitement which she would feel on first being confronted with bigger game.

He allowed a few days to go by to give the animals time to get used to the hide, and when he knew that long enough had passed, he had Lenita woken very early in the morning, much earlier than usual. They went out. To see their way down the track and the trace, Barbosa struck matches as they went. It was as black as pitch. When they reached the *caneleira* it was still dark. The crowns of the trees formed a compact black mass, indistinguishable from the inky sky. Lenita was sleepy and kept yawning. The servant girl was all hunched up, huddled in her shawl.

'It would seem that we have mistimed it today, we have come too early,' said Lenita.

'We have come at just the right time,' Barbosa replied.

'The birds won't start to arrive for another hour at least.'

---

[48] An insectivorous mammal.
[49] Italian: raids, forays.

'Let them come when they will. Today we are not here for the sake of birds.'

'Then for the sake of what?'

'You'll see. Marciana, you stay here. Sit down, and don't make a sound. Now Miss Lenita, come with me.'

'Where are we going?'

'Patience — you'll see.'

The girl, deeply intrigued, let him lead her in docile silence. Barbosa went ahead to show the way; now he gave her his hand, now he held back a branch so that it would not strike her face. They reached the hide.

'After you, Lenita,' he said, politely stepping aside at the door, as if he were inviting her to the buffet in a formal, aristocratic ballroom.

Lenita stepped confidently and resolutely into this dark cave where she could not see a thing.

Barbosa entered behind her, struck a match, showed her the bench and made her sit down. He propped her shotgun on the forked stick, aiming it at the clear ring with the bait, and sat down beside her.

'But, tell me, what is this all about?'

'That is a bait-ring. Now silence, and wait.'

Inside the hut, lined with the dense covering of still green palms, it was relatively comfortable. Lenita, her hands protected by woollen gloves and wrapped in a thick cashmere water-proof, sensed the warmth of Barbosa's body and felt at ease. She inhaled the pure, fresh air of the jungle, breathed the scents of *guarirova*, the irritating emanations of this palm which numbed the brain in mystic lubricity. It was a delight to hear the quiet, monotonous dripping of the dew on the carpet of dead leaves. Time passed unnoticed. Dawn broke. The light filtered down into the jungle, gave colour to the trunks and foliage, lit up the bare brown floor of the bait-ring, where a bright note was struck by the yellow pile of maize.

Suddenly, Barbosa nudged Lenita with his knee.

A small, slim, elegant animal emerged from the jungle and advanced cautiously, extending its slender body. It reached the maize, drew back, hunched itself, fled from the mounds, hid, then reappeared and, still nervous and suspicious, began to eat. Little by little it gained confidence and sat back on its haunches, raising its front paws. Taking a maize stalk into its little hands it began to gnaw with voracious appetite.

Pale, almost swooning, her heart beating furiously, Lenita raised the shotgun by hunter's instinct, aimed and fired.

The shot resounded through the forest, echoing with a dry crack from distant gorges.

The clearing was filled with smoke.

Lenita and Barbosa ran out to see the result of the shot.

Beside the maize lay the animal, its fur ruffled, racked from time to time by a weak spasm, pierced through by the fatal lead.

It was a *cutia*.

On seeing it wounded, prostrate, weakly breathing its last, Lenita's pleasure was so intense that her legs gave way and she fell to her knees, as she looked up at Barbosa with gratitude.

She rose to her feet, laid down the shotgun and picked up the animal, weighing it in both hands. She was hysterical with her triumph, trembling, and shaken by nervous giggles.

'Now let's go back to the hide, there will be more game along shortly,' said Barbosa, scraping earth with his boots over the blood and hairs which lay on the ground. Then he picked up Lenita's gun, presented it to her and offered to carry the *cutia*.

'You take the gun, I'll carry the *cutia*,' she replied.

They settled into the hide again. Lenita loaded her gun, sat down and placed the *cutia* before her, resting her toes on the slim body. She glued vigilant, greedy, covetous eyes on the bait-ring.

She did not have to wait long. There was a crackling of broken twigs and two big, dark shapes appeared one after the other, two enormous wild pigs with white chins. They entered the bait-ring confidently, slowly, majestically, and went straight to the maize, snuffling and rooting with their snouts, clacking their tushes. They stopped, and calmly and carelessly began to eat.

Lenita cocked the shotgun and made to take aim. Barbosa stopped her with a sharp gesture.

'Don't move,' he whispered rapidly in her ear. 'We are in grave danger.'

'In danger?'

The two peccaries continued to eat, champing on the maize without a suspicion of the humans not far away.

Ten minutes passed; to Lenita they seemed like ten anxious centuries.

Slowly and cautiously, as silent as a shadow, Barbosa took Lenita's gun and replaced it with his own, an excellent Pieper 12-bore, with rifled choke barrels.

'Shoot with this,' he whispered, so low that Lenita could hardly hear. 'Don't be afraid, it doesn't kick.'

Lenita drew back both hammers, applying pressure to the triggers so that the sear would not click on the teeth of the hammer nut. She brought the gun to her cheek and, almost without aiming, fired first one barrel and then the other.

The terrifying reports of the heavy charges reverberated through the jungle. All-masking smoke filled the clearing, and there was a strong, agreeable smell of potassium sulphate from the burnt powder.

Lenita was impatient to go out, she could hardly restrain herself. Barbosa held her back.

'Careful!' he said. 'Wait for the smoke to clear. This is no laughing matter, they are *queixadas*.'[50]

'You mean I was shooting at *queixadas*?'

'Yes. Luckily there are only two of them, not a herd.'

'And if there were a herd...?'

'Then we would be lost.'

'Are they that dangerous?'

'In a herd, in the jungle, more dangerous than a jaguar. Give me the gun — I'm going to reload, for safety's sake.'

The smoke cleared slowly. Barbosa and Lenita went out. The earth round the maize was all broken up and there was a lot of blood. From the jungle, not far away, came a snorting sound, a groan of pain.

Barbosa ordered Lenita to stay where she was and walked into jungle towards the sound, his gun cocked and ready to fire. He did not have to go far. A little way in, the two peccaries were lying close together, both hit by Lenita's accurate shots. One was dead, the other was snorting weakly in its death throes.

'*Albo notanda dies lapillo!*'[51] Come here, Lenita, and see your handiwork!' called Barbosa.

Lenita hurried forward, heedless of the branches which lashed her and scratched her face as she ran, and the thorns which tore her clothing. When she arrived at the spot and saw her victims, she quite

---

[50] White-lipped peccaries.
[51] 'A day to be marked with a white stone' Horace. In Roman calendars, days for celebration were marked with a white stone, while a black one indicated misfortune.

lost her head, and in a fit of dizziness she hurled herself on Barbosa with a scream of delight, hugging him frantically. Then she came to her senses. She stepped back in confusion, thoroughly disconcerted, and ran to examine the *queixadas*.

She bent over the dead animal and examined it slowly and carefully: the stiff hackles, the long, hard bristles, stiff ears, smooth snout and little bloodshot eyes; the slanting tushes and the white chin. She pulled off her gloves to press and knead the swollen gland on the rump, squeezing out the whitish, musky liquid.

'You are lucky,' said Barbosa with a smile. 'You have achieved something which few old hunters can boast of.'

'I owe it to you! Thank you.'

There was such tenderness, such feeling in Lenita's voice as she spoke these words that Barbosa felt a shiver run down his spine. It required a violent effort on his part to control himself, to resist the urge to throw himself at the girl and cover her with kisses.

'Then shall we go back to the hide and wait for more game?' he asked.

'No,' Lenita replied. 'There will certainly not be any more *queixadas*, and it would spoil the day and the shot to shoot at smaller game. How will we carry these monsters home?'

'I will send a slave to fetch them with a cart.'

'I want to take the *cutia*, at least.'

'Then we'll take the *cutia*.'

'That smaller peccary won't die — shall we finish it off?'

'It's not worth it; it won't live long. It's very badly wounded.'

'But are they really *queixadas*?'

'Yes, big ones.'

'Good eating?'

'Excellent, even better than *tatetos*.'

'What is the difference between the *queixada* and the *tateto*?'

'The *queixada*, *Dycotyles labiatus*, lives only in virgin jungle; it is bigger and much more ferocious than the *tateto*, *Dycotyles torquatus*,[52] which is small, shy and sometimes lives in the woods. But the distinguishing feature is that the *queixada*, as you see, has a white chin.'

'And that is where the name comes from?'

'Exactly. Now, shall we go?'

---

[52] The smaller and more common collared peccary. In modern taxonomy these two species of peccary are *Tayassu albirostris* and *T. tajacu*.

'To be honest I don't really want to be separated from my magnificent victims — but let's go.'

They went.

The bait-ring remained deserted for some time. Suddenly, daring in its own insignificance, a small rat appeared; it approached without ceremony and started to gnaw the maize, only the germ, the heart of the grain. Then came another, and another, a swarm. A shaft of sunlight pierced the leaves and lit up the pile of loose maize and grainless stalks in a blaze of golden reflections.

Crawling and undulating through the creeping plants of the jungle, pausing here, listening there, a large snake made its way towards the bait-ring. Its back was matt brown, marked with dark, almost black, lozenges. Its head was flat, its nose square-ended, as if cut short, with two closed channels, two false vents. A black line was drawn back from each eye, and faded out on the neck. The tail ended in what looked like a short rosary of flattened, hollow, horny beads, which, as the snake crawled forward, made a slight, almost imperceptible sound, as of crackling parchment.

As it approached, it saw the rats and stopped. Then it began to twist into a spiral, a coil, from which the fearful head emerged attentive, vigilant. There was fascination in the stare of the bright, icy, black eye. The long, thin, vivid, forked tongue flickered swiftly in the air. One of the rodents noticed the reptile, stared at it terror-struck; it curled up into a ball, its hair standing on end, and set up a miserable, pitiful squealing. The others disappeared.

The fascination continued.

The unfortunate rat trembled. It began to move jerkily in irregular, uncoordinated hops. It did not flee, but advanced towards the snake, coming closer and closer. The foul coil suddenly shot out, like a clock-spring escaping from the drum, and struck. The little animal, wounded by the lightning fang, fell on its side. Within a minute it was dead.

Then the snake uncoiled completely, stretched out its full length, opened its huge, gaping mouth and began to devour its prey, dislocating its jaws to allow passage to the relatively large volume of the body...

Then, satiated, gorged, its meal making a visible bulge in its swollen abdomen, it slid slowly and carefully away in search of a retreat, and arriving at the hide it slipped in and coiled up under the wooden seat to begin the comatose sleep of its serpentine digestion.

Lenita was in seventh heaven all day with the memory of her brilliant moment of hunting glory. She had but to close her eyes to see the bait-ring, the *queixadas*. She was pleased with herself — even proud.

Dinner was a cheerful meal.

Baked golden, covered with rounds of lemon, tasty and tempting, the main course was the fillet of one of the *queixadas*. The noblest part, the head, *la hure*,[53] de-boned in masterly fashion by Barbosa, who, like Dumas *père*, was an expert chef, was throned in splendour on a platter, majestic, imposing, fragrant, captivating.

'I will die of indigestion!' exclaimed the Colonel as he served himself one piece after another. 'And it is your fault, Lenita. I haven't eaten wild pig for years! The head is delicious; there's nothing to match it... except the fillet!'

Then, after the coffee, she, Barbosa and the maid went back to the bait-ring.

However hot the day, it is always cool in the jungle. The light is not harsh and piercing as it is in the open country. It is fragmented and attenuated, imparting a velvety softness, a gentle languor, to the outlines of objects. Sounds are deadened, reduced to murmurs. At any time, a sort of vague mysteriousness holds sway there.

Lenita felt happy in this balmy, healthy atmosphere.

To the pleasant, indefinable well-being of the sound digestion of a succulent meal were added pleasures of the mind — in knowing that her love for Barbosa was returned, and in the splendid, incredible, unexpected triumph over two fierce wild animals. It was treachery to have killed them with a gun, in hiding… No! In the terrible struggle for survival any weapon is permitted. Cunning is strength. It is the rifle with the exploding round which makes a man a match for a rhinoceros. Would a man go to attack a rhinoceros without a rifle with an exploding round, to demonstrate his courage? The beasts of the jungle never let a man approach them, they flee as soon as they scent a man nearby; therefore a man can only come within range of them by hiding, concealing himself. So, to be fair, must the man shout to warn them of his presence? Strength is a contraction of muscular fibre, thought is an irritation of the neural cells: why not employ one against the other? In the battle for existence, no matter the weapon used, what matters is — not to be conquered. The victor is always right. The *queixadas* had died. Lenita had triumphed. Once more,

---

[53] French for the head of a boar or other game.

brain had overcome brawn. Those were the facts, the rest counted for nothing.

Barbosa stopped at the foot of the *canaleira* to study some epiphytes which he had found on a rotten branch.

'You won't come, then?' Lenita asked him.

'Not yet. Take Marciana, she can help you with anything you need. There is no danger now. Those were the only *queixadas* — they had become separated from a herd which was living here a few months ago. The administrator knew about them, he had seen them when he went to fell timber.

'Till later, then.'

'Goodbye, I won't be long.'

Lenita went on a little way with Marciana, then told her to wait for orders under a tree, within calling distance. She approached the bait-ring, peering cautiously from a distance. It was deserted.

She entered the hide, sat down, positioned her shotgun and waited. A flock of *urus* was flying nearer; twice she heard their loud, fluting, broken arpeggios close at hand. They appeared, invading the bait-ring. There were twelve of them — some settled down to a dust bath, anxious, dyspeptic, ruffling their feathers, while others started to eat eagerly, greedily.

Lenita made a move to stand up and trod on something soft which yielded under her foot. At almost the same moment she felt something lash her legs and a slight tingling, a mild burning sensation in the point of her left foot.

There was a commotion in the lining of palm leaves at floor level and she heard a rough, rattling sound, nervous and irritating like a dry bean-pod vibrating frantically.

In a corner of the hide, reared up and ready to strike again, was the rattlesnake. The little eyes, fixed and shining like black diamonds, seemed to flash icy lightning. The end of its tail, standing up vertically, vibrated like the striker of an electric bell, like a jet of steam escaping from a narrow tube.

Lenita knew that she was hurt, recognized the danger in which she stood. She bounded out of the hide and rushed to the clear area of the bait-ring.

The *urus* scattered in terror, flying in all directions.

With admirable presence of mind, Lenita sat on the ground, exposed her leg and took off her boot and stocking.

In the lily-white skin of the top of her foot were two short, parallel marks, little more than a centimetre long.

Lenita squeezed them, cleaned away a sort of yellow serum which they contained; she took the ribbon from her braided hair and tied it very tightly round her leg, above the ankle.

Then she shouted for the girl, telling her to call Barbosa urgently.

Barbosa was not long in coming.

When he found Lenita, pale and sitting on the floor of the bait-ring without her gun, her foot bare, he stood dumbfounded, not knowing what to think.

'What's the matter Lenita? What's happened?' he asked anxiously as he approached.

'I've been bitten by a snake.'

'Don't say that! It's no laughing matter.'

'I am quite serious.'

'Where?'

'Here on the foot, look.'

'Do you know what sort it was?'

'Rattlesnake.'

Barbosa went pale and remained stunned for an instant.

But he recovered himself, knelt down, and, taking Lenita's foot between his hands, he examined it closely.

'It shouldn't be much,' he said. 'It hasn't touched a major vein. The precaution of tying up your leg with this ribbon was excellent. Now, no time for modesty; leave it to me, I know what to do.'

He drew a cheroot from his pocket, bit it in half, chewed it and filled his mouth with the tobacco dissolved in saliva. Then he took Lenita's foot again, respectfully, almost adoringly, put it to his mouth and started to suck the wound strongly, steadily and continuously.

He spat, renewed the tobacco and repeated the operation.

'It's curious,' said Lenita, 'I feel nothing, absolutely nothing. It's as if I hadn't been bitten.'

'But are you sure it was a snake, a rattler?'

'Of course! Listen. Can't you hear it?'

In the hide the sinister rattling continued.

Barbosa took his shotgun and cocked it; he went to the hide door, looked in, raised the gun and fired. Then he entered, and came out at once, holding the dead snake up by the tail. It was a fearsome rattlesnake, four or five feet long, very thick; a monster.

'Lenita,' said Barbosa, throwing the reptile down, 'it would be wrong of me to conceal the seriousness of this from you. But the treatment which we have applied almost assures us of success: by tying up the leg promptly you stopped the flow of blood and therefore the absorption of the venom. I sucked the wound to draw out as much venom as was still possible. Do you feel anything now?'

'Just my vision a little blurred.'

'Let's go home. I will follow a rational treatment process and I hope we will soon see you smiling and cheerful back here at the bait-ring. Don't take off or loosen the tie on your leg.'

They went. Twice on the way Lenita felt giddy and almost fell. Barbosa carried her up some of the difficult ascents. Marciana accompanied them, carrying the shotguns. They arrived. Lenita undressed and lay down. She felt cold and sleepy.

Barbosa went to his room and returned with a bottle of rum: he opened it, filled a large cup and made Lenita drink the whole of it down at once.

'Good, we're half way there. Now just keep still, alright?'

Lenita acquiesced with a sad gesture.

Barbosa sat on the edge of the bed, discreetly lifted a corner of the covers, took Lenita's injured foot and undid the ribbon from around the leg. It left a deep, livid ring just above the ankle. The foot was swollen.

He rubbed the skin for a time to restore the circulation, then replaced the tie.

Lenita began to show signs of anxiety and distress.

'My head aches, my vision is all blurred, my thoughts are mixed up.'

'Drink another glass of rum. It is necessary.'

'I will — but listen, tell me the truth: I'm dying, aren't I?'

'No, you're not dying. I'll answer for your life.'

'I'm not dying! You're just saying that to comfort me. I know what ophidic poison is.'

'So do I, that is why I say that you are not dying.'

'Very well. In any case I want to tell you something — come close.'

Barbosa bent his head towards the girl's face.

'It is my conviction that I am dying, and I don't want to die without confiding a secret to you.'

'Tell me Lenita, tell me whatever you wish. Confide in me — I am your friend.'

'I love you, Barbosa. I love you deeply...'

Barbosa was flabbergasted. He controlled himself, bent down and gave Lenita's head a chaste, paternal kiss.

'Poor girl! But you aren't going to die. Won't you drink another glass of rum?'

'Very well — the first has already turned my head.'

'That is the point. Here...'

Lenita sat up, drank with difficulty and fell back heavily on the pillow.

'I'm tired... I'm sleepy...'

She closed her eyes.

Barbosa sat up at her bedside almost the whole night. Every half-hour he loosed the ribbon round her leg to re-establish the circulation for a while, then re-tied it. The girl did not even wake.

She murmured unconnected words in her sleep without regaining consciousness. She swallowed two more glasses of rum at Barbosa's hands, almost by force.

In the early hours she woke and called the maid. Barbosa retired discreetly, and Lenita went back to sleep almost immediately.

In the morning, Barbosa questioned the maid:

'Did Miss Lenita urinate?'

'Yes, Sir.'

'Have you thrown out the urine?'

'No Sir, it's there in the pot, in the night stand.'

'Go and fetch it.'

The maid brought the chamberpot: it was more than half full with dark, bloody urine.

'Did Miss Lenita sweat in the night?'

'I didn't notice, Sir.'

'Go and see. If she did, change her nightdress and bring me the wet one.'

Within ten minutes the maid returned with the nightdress which she had taken off Lenita. It was damp, slightly stained in patches with a washed-out pink.

Lenita awoke at midday.

She was cool and cheerful, and had an appetite.

Barbosa had some chicken broth sent up, thick and filling; he made her take a cup of it, and drink a glass of *vinho velho*.[54]

The Colonel, on hearing what had happened, was thoroughly upset.

'*Vegetalina*. Why didn't you give her *vegetalina*? It's an excellent remedy.'

'Alcohol is an excellent remedy' Barbosa replied. '*Vegetalina* and other specific remedies of that type owe the effect attributed to them to the alcohol in which they are administered.'

'But *vegetalina* has saved a lot of people from the grave.'

'And how do you give *vegetalina*, can you tell me?'

'In strong *cachaça*, twenty-four degrees.'

'There you are then. Lenita did not take *vegetalina* and I consider her out of danger.'

'It seems the rattlesnake didn't have much poison? Was it a small one?'

'It was huge.'

'And Lenita — you think she is out of danger?'

'She had the bright idea of tying up her leg. I sucked the wounds. Little of the poison was absorbed.'

'You sucked the wound? Did you chew tobacco? You haven't got any mouth ulcers have you, or scratches on your tongue?'

'Fortunately my mouth is completely healthy.'

'And what did you give her to drink?'

'First class alcohol. Jamaica rum.'

'Neat?'

'Neat.'

'Hum! I don't know…'

'My treatment was completely rational: I put into practice what I learnt from Paul Bert, who learnt it from Claude Bernard.[55] You know how the circulation works. The haematose blood in the lungs is transferred through the pulmonary vein to the reservoir in the left chambers of the heart: from there it exits through the aorta, and flows through the arterial system, reviving the whole organism; it comes to the capillaries, is transfused and returns through the veins carrying residua. It enters the right auricular of the heart, collects the reparatory elements brought by the sub-clavical veins, passes into the

---

[54] A heavy, sweet wine often served as an aperitif.
[55] Claude Bernard, 1813–1878, French doctor and physiologist, did work on the poison *curare*. Paul Bert, 1833–1886, French physiologist and politician.

right ventricle, is cleaned and re-oxygenated once more in the lungs and so on, unceasingly. So far so good. In the case of any infection with poison, for example a snake-bite, there are three phases, three inevitable *stages*: first, the venom is dissolved in the animal humours present in the wound; second, the venom penetrates the veins and is carried to the heart; third, the venom is brought into contact with the bodily organs via the arterial flow. You know, Father, that what makes any substance *poisonous* is not its quality but its quantity: a milligram of strychnine is not poisonous to a man because, taken all at once, it does not kill. A litre of brandy is poisonous because, taken at once, it will strike him dead. A poison which is eliminated before it has a toxic effect is not poisonous. In the case of a snake-bite, for the venom to have a fatal effect, its elimination must be disproportional, it must be slower than the absorption; there must be an accumulation in the blood. Very well: the venom is in the wound, but it cannot go up to the heart, it is stopped by the tourniquet. This state cannot be prolonged, gangrene will set in. It is essential to undo the tie and allow the blood to go up, carrying the venom. You untie it and leave it for a little, but in such a way that not enough venom enters the bloodstream to produce a lethal effect — and so that it is eliminated before another quantity enters which, added to the first, can produce that effect. So the tourniquet is loosened and re-tied, loosened and re-tied, until all the venom has passed through the body and been eliminated without causing death. Alcohol excites the nerves, accelerates the flow of the blood; it therefore helps with the elimination.'

'And are there examples of cures effected by this process?'

'Countless. Claude Bernard saved animals whenever he chose, which he himself had infected with arrows dipped in *curare*. In the Province of Rio, a friend of mine was bitten by a huge *surucucú* and I saved him by following this treatment.

'So Lenita?...'

'Is my second patient. I consider that she is as safe now as she was yesterday before she was bitten.'

'Can I see her?'

'Of course.'

They went into the room. Lenita was sitting up in bed, her legs crossed Chinese-style under the covers. Happy and radiant, she had that air of triumph common to all patients who have recovered from a serious illness. A piece of bright white cambric, folded into a strip, bound her head like a diadem, bringing out the brilliance of her eyes, the black hair, the golden pallor of her face. The wide, soft folds of a high-cut nightdress of raw silk barely concealed the firm line of her breasts.

'So, you're ready for the next adventure!' said the Colonel. 'You've had a lucky escape… That's what comes of hunting. You might have been killed!'

'But I wasn't.'

'Hasn't it made you afraid of the jungle?'

'No, it has made me more experienced. I shall be careful to keep my eyes open in future: I shall not put my foot down anywhere without looking carefully first. And really it was more the fright. You see I had a slight headache, I felt weak all over, and sleepy: but pain, real pain, no.'

'You were lucky, you found a good doctor.'

Lenita turned her soft glance on Barbosa, brimming with gratitude.

Chapter 14

It seemed that the snake venom had tainted Lenita's blood.

She was seized with sudden fits of spiritual lassitude, just as when she had first arrived at the *fazenda*.

She gave up hunting, she gave up reading; her thirst for science was extinguished.

At any moment she would sit in the hammock, or a rocking-chair, and sink into a day-dream. She ate little — almost nothing.

At times she would lean over the table, lay down her head and take a pencil, a flower, any small object, and turn it and turn it in her hands, beating a strange rhythm, for long periods — with unseeing eyes and expressionless face, as if she were a million miles removed from earthly matters.

Barbosa for his part became more reserved; Lenita's confession of love had intimidated him.

Insensibly, he had allowed himself to be caught in a trap which he had not expected, not even suspected.

He found himself in an extremely awkward position. He loved Lenita madly, to perdition; he knew that she loved him; he had heard it from her own lips. Now what? Either to make a clean break, pack his bags and sail for Europe, or become the girl's acknowledged lover. A sentimental, platonic flirtation, in the circumstances, would be the height of the ridiculous.

And Barbosa spent most of his time in visits and cards with their neighbours, he who before never used to play, never visited anyone.

He walked out in the jungle with his shotgun, but the gun was a pretext. He never shot anything.

One afternoon, near sunset, he sat down to rest at the foot of a white fig, in the heart of the virgin jungle, and looking up automatically; he saw an enormous *quati-mundé* peering down at him from the fork of a branch, grimacing with its long, sharp snout. As if that was not temptation enough, there was a loud clattering of wings and a huge *macuco* came in to land on the fig-tree, directly above the quati. It alighted, settled on a branch, shook its feathers, made itself comfortable, hunched its neck and gave three successive, regular, high-pitched cheeps. Barbosa paid no attention to either the animal or the bird. His shotgun remained untouched between his knees.

Before his eyes, as it were in a beatific vision, hovered the image of a foot, Lenita's foot, white, satiny, tiny, with transparent pink nails and bluish veins.

And he had kissed this foot, more, he had sucked it long and slowly, holding in his hand the adorable heel, round, pink, with very white marks left by the pressure of his fingers.

He could taste the savour of the fine, velvety skin, menaced by death but full of life. It was as if his lips had a memory of their own, recalled the sensation.

And the light, paternal kiss which he had placed on her head when she confessed her love for him. He could still breathe the natural perfume of her hair, the fresh, milky, healthy breath, as from the mouth of a new-born calf.

Why not accept this love which was imposed, given, offered? He had not sought Lenita, she had come to meet him, conscious of the situation, knowing that he was married and could never make her his lawful wife.

And frankly, with the chastest prudence, she had made the confession which no woman ever wants to be the first to make. It was no jest — it had not been a moment for jesting.

What harm would it do the world if they, a man and a woman in love, were joined to one another, possessed one another, enjoyed one another?

He could not marry Lenita? What did that matter? What is marriage nowadays but a sociological institution, in process of evolution like everything else that has to do with living creatures, tolerably immoral and thoroughly ridiculous? Marriage in future should not be this stupid, draconian contract, based on a solemn promise to do exactly what cannot be done. Man, precisely because he occupies the highest rung on the biological ladder, is essentially versatile, changeable. To mortgage an uncertain, no, an improbable future, in the knowledge that the mortgage is worthless, is anything in the world but moral. Eternal love is only for mawkish poetry. Marriage without lawful, regulated, honourable divorce for both parties is a boiler without a safety valve, it must burst. A man arrays himself in his formal coat, a woman dresses herself up and decks herself with symbolic flowers: and off they both go to church, in solemn pomp, with a numerous accompaniment, for what? To announce in public, in the presence of whomever wishes to see and hear, with tinkling of bells and sounding of trumpets, that he wishes to copulate with her, that she wishes to copulate with him, that there are no objections and that the relatives get on well together... How pretty! And the staring crowd of onlookers, young and old, men and women, screwing up their eyes and laughing to show off their white teeth, digging each other with malicious elbows, whispering obscenities! It would be ridiculous if it were not horrible, dirty.

Love is the child of the tyrannical, fatal need of every organism to reproduce, to pay its *debt to its ancestors* according to the Brahmaic formula. The word *love* is a euphemism to soften a little the animal truth of the word *heat*. In physiological truth, *love* and *heat* come down to the same thing. The primordial origin of love is, as biologists say, in the elective affinity of two different cells, or better, of two cells with different electrical charges. The astonishing complexity of the human organism converts this primitive affinity, which should always result in offspring, into a battle of nerves which, if frustrated or badly managed, produces the wrath of Achilles, the excesses of Messalina,[56] the ecstasies of Santa Teresa. There is no resisting love, surrender is the only course. Nature is irresistible and love is nature. The ancients had a clear intuition of the truth when they symbolised in a beautiful and implacably vindictive goddess, Venus Aphrodite, this snare which enmeshes beings, this life-giving soul.

Lenita had offered herself to him; very well, he would become Lenita's lover.

And Barbosa stood up fortified, strengthened, like a man who has come to a definite decision, and walked rapidly homewards.

When he arrived it was almost night, and already dark.

He entered his room, laid down the shotgun and cartridge bag, struck a match, lit a candle and washed his hands.

He went out.

In the corridor, outside the door of the ante-room, he bumped into someone: Lenita.

'Oh!' he exclaimed.

Their hands seemed to seek one another in the darkness, they met and enlaced.

Barbosa pulled Lenita towards him, made to kiss her on the lips, but his courage failed him, and he kissed her on the head again.

Lenita abandoned, surrendered herself, nerveless and unresisting.

It was quite dark in the corridor: Barbosa could not see the black flame of voluptuousness swirling in the girl's eyes; he could not see her pale face, her red, swollen lips panting, begging for kisses; he could not see the languorous lolling of her neck.

---

[56] Wife of the emperor Claudius known for her promiscuity.

His resolution weakened, yielded: Barbosa felt his courage, his desire, even his virility disappear. Meanwhile his heart beat wildly, like a seminarian finding himself alone for the first time with a prostitute.

Suddenly, he abruptly pushed Lenita away from him, and fled in a frenzy.

A desolate, pained sob sounded in the darkness of the corridor.

Dinner that evening was a strained affair. Barbosa did not look at Lenita, nor she at him. They ate, or rather pretended to eat, in silence.

'This girl needs to take some medicine,' said the Colonel, noticing Lenita's dejection and almost total lack of appetite. 'She hasn't been the same since that business with the snake. If you had given her *vegetalina* it would have been a different matter.'

Tea was served: when they had drunk, Barbosa rose, bid his father goodnight, took his leave of Lenita in a subdued, ceremonious, saturnine voice, calling her 'Madam'.

He withdrew.

Lenita talked a little longer with the Colonel. She followed, or pretended to follow the conversation, making observations, asking a mass of questions, feigning a deep interest. Suddenly she would let out a strong, inappropriate exclamation, totally out of context. Then she would come to her senses and try to justify what she had said; she became mixed up and confused. She started as if pricked with a pin. She blushed, turned pale, her voice took on a strange timbre.

'You know what, my girl,' said the Colonel, 'Go and lie down, you are not well. If I'd not seen that you hardly ate a thing, I would say that your dinner didn't agree with you. Off you go — go to bed, try to sleep.'

Lenita obeyed without demur.

She went to her room.

She took a warm bath and lay soaking for a long time, but it did not help to calm her nerves, quite the reverse. Her skin rose in goose-pimples at the passing contact of the sponge, the touch of her own hands; the tepid water excited her as if it were the contact of another human being.

She got out of the bath, dried herself with a big, velvety towel, put on a white nightdress of very fine cambric and lay down on top of the covers, fully extended on her back, her fingers linked behind the back of her head, with one leg crossed over the other.

The soft, semi-transparent cambric followed the sculpted lines of her bust, her belly, her thighs, and all this whiteness of her skin and the material was heightened by the contrast with the dark red damascene of the bedspread. The minutes slipped past.

From her room Lenita could hear the slow, measured ticking of the old French clock in the ante-room.

It struck ten, then eleven, then midnight. Every strike of the hammer on the little bell sounded very distinct, very vibrant.

Lenita tossed and turned in her bed, wide awake, unable to sleep.

A mordant obsession rose from the periphery of her body, constricting her heart, making her head spin.

She felt hot and cold, her skin tingled, there was a ringing in her ears.

Sucking the wounds made by the fangs of the rattlesnake, Barbosa had extracted one venom from her body, but replaced it with another. Not for a moment had Lenita ceased to feel the strong, warm, extended suction of his lips around the wounds on the top of her foot. The strange, delicious, contradictory sensation produced by this suction remained present, alive; more than that, it multiplied and spread. It was a tingling which spiralled up her legs, caressed her belly, titillated her breasts, set her lips on fire.

She loved Barbosa, desired Barbosa, ached for Barbosa.

To wait for morning: one! two! three! four! five! six hours! To hear the ticking of the clock, slow, measured, regular, unvarying, metallic, monotonous, pitiless. To hear it sixty times a minute, three thousand, six hundred times an hour, twenty-one thousand, six hundred times in the six hours remaining until dawn? Impossible!

She stood up and, barefoot in her nightdress, unconscious, crazed, opened the door; she crossed the hall, opened the next door, went out into the ante-room, down the corridor, and stopped outside Barbosa's door, listening.

She heard nothing.

Within the room, as without, reigned a profound silence, broken only by the violent beating of her own heart.

She put her ear to the keyhole — nothing.

Her shoulder leant lightly against the door, which yielded and opened with a faint creak.

A gust of warm air, saturated with the aroma of Havana cheroot, brushed over her face, her breasts, her bust almost completely exposed by the low-cut nightdress.

Lenita lost her head completely, and entered. Creeping on tip-toe, slipping silent and ghost-like, she went to the side of Barbosa's bed.

She leant over, putting her hand on the bed-head for support; her head hung just above the breast of the sleeper, she listened to his regular breathing, smelt the masculine smell of his body, felt the warmth off his skin.

She stood for minutes in this drowsy atmosphere. Suddenly, her supporting hand slipped, she fell heavily across the bed.

Barbosa shuddered and woke with a start. He sat up, stretched out his hands, found and seized her, asking in amazement:

'Who is it? Who is it?'

The girl's warm, silky skin, the smoothness of the cambric which covered her in part, the perfume of *peau d'Espagne* which wafted from her body, left him no room for doubt; but he refused the evidence of his senses, could not believe it. He found it absurd, monstrous, impossible that Lenita should be in his room at such an hour, in a state of such barely covered nakedness.

And yet it was real, there she was: he felt her warm, firm flesh, ran his fingers over her skin, goose-pimpled with desire, listened to the effervescence of her blood, the pulsing of her heart.

A host of disordered ideas whirled confusedly in his excited brain; reason abandoned him, desire overcame him, the triumphant prompting of the *flesh*.

He sat up suddenly on the edge of the bed without releasing the girl, pulled her to him, clasped her to his breast, then, supporting her head with his left hand, nervous and brutal, he covered her mouth with his, pressed his rough moustaches against her smooth lips, drank in her breath.

Lenita was seized with an inexplicable sensation of terror, tried to flee, made a violent effort to disentangle, to release herself.

It was the fear of the male, that terrible physiological fear which assaults every woman, every female, in the prelude to the first copulation.

Vain attempt!

Barbosa's robust arms restrained her. His kisses multiplied on her face, her eyes, her neck: and these ardent, hungry kisses burned her skin, turned her blood to glowing lava, whipping her nerves, torturing her flesh.

Growing bolder, more uncontrolled by the minute, he moved down her throat, reached the firm, swollen, panting breasts. He mouthed and kissed them, at first respectfully, fearfully, like one committing an act of sacrilege; then insolently, lasciviously, bestially, like a satyr. In growing exaltation he sucked and bit the erect nipples.

'Stop! Let me alone! Please, not like this!' Lenita resisted, imploring him brokenly, panting in her efforts to escape, but at the same time captive to an invincible need of surrender, abandonment.

Suddenly her legs gave way, her arms hung down, her head slumped; her resistance ceased as she yielded herself up to him, weak, limp, passive. Barbosa raised her in his powerful arms, laid her on the bed, lay down beside her and drew her to him. He covered her smooth breasts with his broad chest, glued his lips to hers.

She let him do what he would, unconscious, almost swooning, hardly responding to the frenetic kisses which devoured her.

Time passed.

Barbosa could not believe what was happening.

Disillusioned with women, divorced from his wife, worn out, misanthropic, he had abandoned the world, retired with his books and his scientific instruments to a corner of the jungle, a *fazenda* in the *sertão*. He had abandoned society, changed his habits, conserving his hygiene, the cult of the body, the unpretentious need to dress, as the only relics of his past. He spent his life in study and meditation; he was achieving a state of quietude, the peace of the spirit of which Plautus speaks, which is found only in a sincere, unchanging dedication to books, to the absent and the dead. And suddenly fate throws in his path a virgin, a beautiful, intelligent young woman, educated, noble and wealthy. And this woman falls in love with him, forces him to love her in return, captivates and destroys him. And more, against all expectations, converting the improbable, the absurd into reality, she comes to his room, wakes him and surrenders herself to him… He is holding her in his arms, limp, languid, gnawed by desire; he draws her towards him, kisses her…

And… he can do nothing more!

Not that he is held back by prejudice or fear of the consequences; he has no prejudices, is past fearing consequences. What stops him is a momentary nervous exhaustion, an unexpected physical inability.

He seeks in vain, through the concentration of willpower, to give tone to the nervous fibre, to strengthen his organism…

He is keenly aware of the ridiculousness of the situation; desperate, bathed in sweat, his hands turning to ice, weeping even.

He moved apart from Lenita, demented, insane, tearing at his chest with his nails.

'I can't, I can't!' he exclaimed, he howled in despair.

A reversal occurred in their roles: confronted with this sudden coolness, this cessation of his caresses, the cause of which she could not understand or even suspect, in a fury of eroticism which changed her nature and converted her into a shameless bacchante, a debauched creature, Lenita clutched Barbosa, embraced him, twined her arms about him, her legs, like an octopus clinging to its prey; her open mouth, panting and wet, sought his mouth; with an instinctive refinement of sensuality she bit his lips, kissed the polished surface of his teeth, sucked his tongue…

And her pleasure was revealed in her accelerated breathing, her short, hot exhalations. An intense, frenzied pleasure, but… still incomplete, flawed.

Gasping for breath, Barbosa was trying to get up, to find his pistol and blow out his brains.

Little by little, a reaction set in.

Barbosa felt the blood pumping less agitatedly through his veins, a sweet warmth spreading through his limbs, physical desire awakening, dominant and imperative.

He recovered from his passing weakness, felt himself strong, potent, a man.

With the irresistible impetus of the male in heat, and more, of the man who needs to make up for a humiliating weakness, he took back the role of the assailant, pressed the girl in his arms, buried his head in the silky, perfumed waves of her hair, which had come untied…

'Lenita!'

'Barbosa!'

A victorious kiss choked in Lenita's throat the cry of pain of a virgin losing her maidenhead….

Followed an unrestrained, shuddering tempest of fierce caresses, in which the bodies came together, melted into one another, became one; in which flesh penetrated flesh; in which shiver responded to shiver, kiss to kiss, bite to bite.

From this organic undulation escaped little, suffocated cries, whimpers of pleasure, interspersed with the short gasps of their exhausted panting.

Then a long sigh followed by a long silence.

Then a renovation, a renewal of the struggle, fiery, blazing, bestial, insatiable.

A glimmer of tenuous light traced the crack between the shutters.

It was the dawn.

'Let me go! Let me go, Barbosa! I must leave, it's dawn, it's getting light.'

'No, no! Not yet! That's not daylight, it's the moon.'

'I'm going! Let me go.'

With a violent effort, Lenita escaped from the bed, from Barbosa's arms.

Her indecisive figure was silhouetted for a moment in the frame of the open door. She disappeared.

Barbosa stood up, dressed rapidly and went out. He locked the door, took the key and put it in his pocket.

From her room Lenita heard him, counted his heavily echoing footsteps.

She was feverish, her head was on fire; she felt numbed and dizzy. Before her eyes bright discs kept appearing, with a nucleus which grew and changed in colour from dark green to coppery-red; her throat was dry, her mouth was sticky.

In Barbosa's deserted room, the glimmer of light which filtered between the shutters fell on the disordered bed: the whiteness of the rumpled sheets was brightly spotted with a few fresh, wet, crimson bloodstains.

Chapter 15

'What a beautiful day!' exclaimed the Colonel, standing in the door which led out to the yard. 'Settled weather, for sure! Jacinto!'

'Yes, Massah!' An old negro answered his summons.

'Where are they working today?'

'Gone to cut rice, yes Massah.'

'Where's Manduca?'

'Young massah had the skewball saddled, and went into town, yes Massah.'

The Colonel took a deep draught of the fresh, pure air of the resplendent morning. He had slept all night, not so much as a twinge, and he felt in fine fettle. He would have liked to spread himself, to converse.

'Just today when I'm longing for a chat and Manduca takes off — and as for Lenita, she's still abed! What a thing! I shall indulge myself and take a turn up to the coffee.'

He ordered them to saddle a quiet old mare, a walking horse, 'a hammock' as he said, and went out to visit the coffee plantation — something he seldom did, not above once or twice a year.

When he returned it was nearly midday. He asked for Barbosa, who had not arrived; for Lenita — she was still in bed. He was hungry, so he ordered the table to be laid, and while he was waiting he went to Lenita's room and knocked on the door.

'What's the matter?' he asked. 'Are we feeling unwell?'

'Not unwell, just sleepy,' the girl replied.

'Were you asleep?'

'I woke when you knocked.'

'Look, come and keep me company. I don't know where Manduca has gone. I haven't had luncheon yet and I don't want to eat by myself.'

'I'll be there in no time.'

'Then I'll wait. Don't be long, I'm starving!'

Half an hour later, Lenita appeared. She was deathly pale: her eyelids were red, her eyes dull, with big dark rings. She was wrapped in a shawl. From time to time she shivered. She sat at the table, half turned away, broken and languid.

'I hope you're better tomorrow!' exclaimed the Colonel on seeing her! 'Looks as if you spent the night in the cemetery. What's the matter?'

'A slight indisposition.'

'Hmm! I could see that coming last night. Ah, girls, girls! As long as they don't get married… What would you like? A little yam *mingau*[57] perhaps?'

'No, thank you.'

'Look at these vegetables…'

'No, thank you.'

'A piece of cold ham?'

'Ham? Yes, please; but just a little.'

The Colonel served her a long, pink slice, marbled with veins of white fat.

Lenita sprinkled it with ground salt and ate heartily.

'You like salty things, eh? Just as I was saying… Another little slice?'

Lenita accepted; she asked for ginger-ale and drank a whole glassful.

She talked with the Colonel for a couple of hours. As the afternoon wore on she wilted, overcome by irresistible somnolence.

She went to her room and slept. She rose at dusk. As she came out of her room she met Barbosa, who, standing by a pier table, pretended to be examining a statuette.

'Good evening, Lenita,' he said, his voice trembled. He appeared shy and uncomfortable.

The girl did not speak; with a nervous movement she took his head between her hands bent it down, kissed it avidly, extravagantly, on the crown, masking, burying her face in the short, slightly curly hair.

'Lenita,' whispered Barbosa in a low voice, tenuous as a breath, don't come to my room again, it is dangerous. Someone might see you or find you. I will come to yours, that will be better.'

'The girl sleeps here.'

'It's easy to send her away under some pretext. Leave the doors shut.'

They went to the dining room.

'The Colonel had already had the lamp lit. He was standing by the table, reading his correspondence, which had arrived from town a few minutes earlier.

'Look, Lenita,' he said, 'here are your newspapers, and a letter. You should read the letter at once — it will interest you.'

'Oh yes? How do you know?'

---

[57] A sort of porridge given to children and convalescents.

'The writing on the envelope is the same as on this one for me. Read it.'

'What can it be?' she wondered in annoyance as she tore open the envelope with a tired gesture. She unfolded the sheet of paper, read without betraying the slightest emotion, with absolute indifference. Then passed the open letter to the Colonel.

'Well!' she exclaimed, dragging her voice in distaste.

'Well what?' asked the Colonel.

'Read for yourself.'

'Isn't it from Dr. Mendes Maia?'

'It is.'

'And what do you say to him?'

'I... I... have nothing at all to say.'

'It's clear what you want. Silence means...'

'Not always assent. Dr. Mendes Maia has wasted his time, his rhetoric, his paper, his ink and his stamp. I'm not going to marry him.'

'Is it a proposal of marriage?' asked Barbosa anxiously.

'Formal.'

'And who is this Dr. Mendes Maia?'

'This Dr. Mendes Maia is a bachelor at law, from the north; he has done his four years and is in the court waiting for an appointment as a judge here in the province.

'And where did you meet him?'

'In Campinas. We met at a ball, in the *Semanal Club*, it must be three years ago. He danced with me, paid court to me for two hours and now he is asking for my hand in marriage.'

'Do you know him too, Father?'

'Yes, I do. He came this way with a cousin who wanted to buy a coffee plantation. He had a recommendation from São Paulo; he even put up here for a night.'

'What sort of man is he?'

'He is a bachelor at law like most bachelors at law. He seems a good enough person. For me, to be frank, he has one capital failing: he comes from the north. For the rest, nothing to say. Lenita, what am I to reply to the man?'

'A fine question! Reply that I have no desire to marry, that I am deeply grateful for the honour of his proposal, that sort of thing, a polite refusal.'

'Would it not be worth thinking it over a little before deciding the matter so abruptly, without a second thought?'

'There is nothing to think about. I do not want to marry him.'

'Listen, according to my old friend Santa Cruz Chaves, who sent me this other letter, the boy has all that is required of a good match: he is intelligent, honest, well mannered, hard-working, economical, a good catholic and lots of other things. He did his four years in practice as a prosecutor and town magistrate, and now he is waiting for a judge's vacancy, as you say; and is likely to get it, because he is on good terms with Cotegipe and is a protegé of MacDowel. And he isn't short of a penny.'

'It may be a tempting match, very, but I am not going to be caught.'

'Listen, it's not a life and death matter, no blood has been spilt; think first and answer later.'

'There is nothing to think about.'

'These girls! Why rush into a decision, when there is time to think, to weigh up all the pros and cons?'

'The answer now or in a year's time is the same: I don't want to.'

'My girl, never say 'never'.'

'And never is a long time. All the same, I don't want to.'

'Very well, very well. You don't want to. Tomorrow we'll send the refusal, and Dr. Mendes Maia will have to lump it.'

Chapter 16

Lenita had sent the maid away and slept alone in her room. The Colonel didn't like it, couldn't understand it. It was dangerous — she might fall ill, have an attack in the night, with no one to look after her.

No, Lenita replied: she was quite alright, there was no fear of an attack; besides, the girl snored, and that stopped her from sleeping.

Barbosa arrived at about eleven o'clock at night; quietly, stepping with care, he entered the sitting room and locked the door from the inside.

The carefully oiled hinges worked easily, with a smooth, light action, without the slightest creak.

The lock was of the old Portuguese make, with coinciding holes in the latches. To prevent anyone spying at the keyhole to see what was happening in the room, improbable as this was, Barbosa hung his hat from the key.

In this absolute and perfect liberty, he was not content only with the material pleasure of possessing Lenita. He desired the mental sin of the intellect, the *mala mentis gaudia*[58] of which Virgil speaks; he wanted to contemplate, to feast his eyes on the superb form of the young woman, now in all the splendour of her glowing nudity, now brought out by the accessories and extravagances of fashion.

He undressed her, placed her in the pose of the *Vénus de Milo*, arranged her arms as the experts conjectured that those of the statue must have been; he wound a sheet about her hips, ruffled it into suggestive folds and artistic drapery.

Then he would tear off this last covering, change her position: lifting her bust, advancing the arch of her chest, making the insolent profile of her firm, erect breasts stand out.

Using a powerful reflector, he directed and focused the white light from a Belgian lamp so that it fell on the girl like a shroud of smooth, lively reflections, scientifically combined.

He moved away, came closer, looked, studied, took pleasure in Lenita like Pygmalion in Galatea or Michelangelo in Moses.

The moment came when he could contain himself no longer: with the hoarse, grating, suffocated cry of a rutting goat he threw himself down, and she with him, and they fell together on a sofa, on the floor, clasping, biting, devouring one another.

At times he made Lenita do up her hair, put on her corsets, deck herself in flowers, put on gloves, with all the caprices, all the

---

[58] The *'wicked joys of the mind'* from *Aeneid* Bk 6.

impertinence of a lioness of style preparing herself for a society ball, a diplomatic *soirée*.

He assisted her, served as her chambermaid, proud and radiant.

All this apparatus of femininity, all this expansion of gaiety, was for him, for him alone, for no one else.

He felt something of the exclusivist, egoistic pleasure of King Ludwig of Bavaria, attending in an empty theatre, alone, as sole spectator, one of Wagner's operas, majestically produced, divinely sung by first class artists.

He adored the warm, perfumed smoothness of Lenita's naked skin; with a refinement of lubriciousness, he loved to press her hands through kid or suede gloves. He loved the contact of these warm hands through the mesh of netted silk mittens; to feel the life in her body through the soft roughness of lace, between the relief flowers of tulle.

Before long, their clandestine nightly unbuttonings between four walls ceased to satisfy him: he sought a wider frame for his living tableaux, a more spacious stage for his fleshly *mises-en-scène*, desired love in the open air, in daylight, in total liberty. On the pretext of hunting, he went out with Lenita into the depths of the forest.

While they were on the way, he let her go ahead, remaining a few paces behind to watch the agitated threshing of her heels under the rosy hem of her light country dress.

This continuous, swirling movement of her skirts, billowing up to blend into the sway of her hips, caused in him a strange and most singular excitement.

When in the forest he came across a deep grotto, a dark ravine, a clearing festooned with creepers and bamboos, he would stop.

By an old trunk, at the foot of the still low, emerald-green fan of a young palm-tree, far below the reach of a cluster of sunbeams, he would pose the naked girl, playing the artist with delight, with the expertise of a practiced libertine, setting off the whiteness of her light-bathed skin against the green ground of the forest submerged in shadow. Lenita lent herself to all this with the docility of a complacent queen, a satisfied goddess. She accepted his adoration, was content to receive the cult of idolatry of which her flesh was the object.

Barbosa looked and looked, walking around her; the concentric circles which he described became tighter and tighter, like those of a goshawk around its prey; he reached her, knelt, and trembling, his breath coming in short pants, he kissed the pink nails and white skin of her feet, straightened up, raised himself boldly, brushed his lips over her rounded thighs, rested his head against her smooth belly, his eyes half closed, inhaling, drinking in the healthy, provocative emanations of the excited female flesh.

Once, in the heart of the jungle, Michelangelo's *Aurora*, which he had seen at the tomb of the Medicis, suddenly came into his mind. The shape of a broken piece of ground was the idea which, by an accident of association, triggered his memory.

Nearby there was an old tree covered in moss. He collected armfuls, created a mound to pad and carpet the formation which had reminded him of the Florentine marble.

Nervously, brutally, he undressed Lenita. He did not unbutton or unhook her, he tore buttons off and burst hooks. When she was naked, he made her recline on the moss; he bent her left leg, resting the foot on a ledge of rock, then bent her left arm so that the hand, abandoned, just brushed the shoulder with the fingertips. He straightened her right arm and leg in a soft, loose line, contrasting with the strong, angular line, full of movement, of the other side.

He stepped down, lay on his front, and crawling like a lizard............................

Lenita swooned in a spasm of pleasure ....
....

One night Barbosa did not come to Lenita's room.

The girl did not sleep for an instant, racked with anxiety. In the early hours she got up, not worrying about the possibility of someone seeing her or finding her, taking no precautions; she went to Barbosa's room, pushed the door open and entered.

The wick of the almost completely spent candle was sinking in a pool of melted wax, which had accumulated in the holder of the candlestick. The flame flickered and trembled, now lighting up the whole room, now disappearing, almost submerging everything in darkness.

Barbosa was lying on his back on the bed, pressing his hands to his temples, groaning. Lenita leant over him.

'What's the matter? What is it?' she asked.

'Nothing. It's my migraine. But you must go, someone may come, it's nearly daybreak.'

'Go? And leave you alone when you are suffering? How little you know me!'

'I do know you, very well. I would not send you away if your presence were necessary, even useful. But there's nothing you can do for me. This is no illness, just discomfort. I am not sick, just suffering pain.'

'I want to stay. I cannot see you in pain without at least trying to relieve it.'

'You will do nothing but upset me and make the pain worse. It will pass, it just takes time, that's all. Go, I beg you, go.'

Lenita went, very annoyed.

These migraines of Barbosa's were horrible.

They began with a dull headache. Little by little he succumbed to an inexplicable irritation with and on account of everything. His strength dwindled and failed, his face became pale, the pupil of the right eye dilated.

Any movement became painful, any effort impossible. Fatally, inevitably, he had to go to bed. A cold sweat covered his body, bathed his forehead. In his right temple, swollen and tumescent, the temporal artery pulsed: the eyeball contracted, shrunk, was sensitive to the slightest pressure as if it had been bruised, trodden on. At the top of his head was a point of pain, where it felt as if a spike had been driven. Every pulsation, every surge of blood in the arteries was a hammering which seemed to make his head burst, to drive the spike deeper. His stomach swelled with bile. He felt ravenous hunger, an imperious need for food, but the very idea of swallowing anything exacerbated all his sufferings. The retina was filled with flashes, subjective points of light which circled like flies; the slightest sound, as if magnified by an infernal microphone, became a clatter, a cataclysm of noise and pain in his hypersensitive ears. He could not think or concentrate. If someone had come at such a moment to tell Barbosa that a fire was destroying his precious library, that his parents were perishing in the flames, he would not have been able to do a thing or make the slightest effort; his willpower was annihilated.

And this unspeakable suffering, this dreadful torture, always lasted until the next night.

Dawn broke.

As soon as the doors were opened, and the *fazenda* came to life, Lenita returned to Barbosa's room, sat beside his bed-head and enquired solicitously what she could do, what was of any help on these occasions.

Nothing, there was nothing at all to be done, Barbosa repeated impatiently; this was a special, hypersensitive state of the nerves, which only went over with time, and he would be better in the evening.

Lenita, with the ineffable touch, the special knack which women have for nursing, arranged the pillows and the bolster for him in such a way as to give him relief; she went to the cupboard and searching among the thousand and one bottles found one almost full of syrup of chloral, brought it and, almost by force, made him take two big, brimming soup-spoons of it.

Then she felt his feet; finding them cold she sent for a hot water bottle, put it beneath them wrapped in a towel, and covered the whole with a blanket, so skilfully that he was hardly incommoded, hardly felt the movements.

Barbosa's groans died away to a sort of indistinct, feverish whimpering. They ceased, he slept.

He slept long, two hours or more.

The girl never left his side for a moment. Sitting motionless at the head of the bed, she watched him sleep in silence.

Suddenly he awoke, sat up quickly and made a sign, an impatient, irritated gesture, ordering her to retire.

Lenita did not obey.

Barbosa, pale, his features contorted, bent over and opened the night-stand in clumsy haste. He pulled out the chamber-pot, put it beside him on the bed and knelt.

Abdomen, stomach, diaphragm, oesophagus contracted in a violent nausea. The zigomatic muscles stretched the discoloured, sunken cheeks, and a jet of frothing, yellow bile shot into the chamber-pot, colouring the sides with sticky splashes.

Another jet followed, and another and another; the bile flowed easily, no longer yellow or frothy, but green, liquid, even beautiful in its transparent purity.

Lenita, with profound pain traced on her features, supported his soaking head.

Exhausted, Barbosa fell heavily back among the pillows, groaned a little, and went back to sleep.

Lenita had the chamber-pot taken away, washed and brought back. Then she reassumed her post beside the patient, watching lovingly over his calm sleep.

When she was called for luncheon she went out on tiptoe, without the slightest sound.

A circumstantial narration of his son's indisposition led the Colonel to remark that it did not cause him concern: the boy had suffered from migraine since childhood, and had even become better with age, the attacks were becoming less frequent.

Lenita returned to the room.

Around midday Barbosa awoke. He felt fine, completely recovered; he was hungry and sent for something to eat.

Chapter 17

The new cane milling had started some time ago. It was almost halfway through when a disaster occurred. A black boy got caught in the drums of the mill and his arm was crushed.

When he saw the unfortunate child caught and being drawn in by the slow, implacable turning of the insensate mechanism, his father, the negro mill-master, took up a steel weigh-beam which he found to hand and thrust it between the teeth of the drums.

There was a tremendous clashing of metal, the loud clanging of breaking ironwork, and the mill stopped.

The boy's life was saved but the mill was useless. Drums, axles, bearings, everything was shattered.

It was a calamity, the very devil, this disaster in the middle of the harvest, exclaimed the Colonel in dismay. Not for the little black: he was free, thanks to 28 September,[59] it didn't matter if he was crippled, that was no great loss. The disaster was the interruption to the milling, just when everything was going so well, at the worst possible time. He did not want to repair the mill; for years he had been intending to rebuild the whole thing; and rebuild he would, although the rest of the crop would go down the drain.

It was agreed that Barbosa would go to Ipanema the next morning to talk to Dr. Mursa about plans and dimensions for the new machine which they needed urgently, within a few days.

Lenita, when she heard of this journey, was startled and paled, almost swooned. She remembered how she had suffered with Barbosa's trip to Santos, when he was not yet her lover, when she was not even sure that she loved him.

How would it be now, when things were on a very different footing? An unspeakable, impossible, hellish torture.

But it was not.

Lenita helped Barbosa to prepare for his journey, without feeling in the least what she had felt the last time. The unbridled, lubricious extravagances to which he gave way on their last night together upset her, mortified her even.

She was amazed at the sudden, abrupt transition which had occurred in her spirit. She felt cold, indifferent, almost annoyed. She found him gross, vulgar, impertinent, ridiculous, a bore.

At the moment of departure she pressed his hand; watched him mount his horse, twitch the reins, move off slowly in a cloud of dust

---

[59] Under the Law of the Free Womb of 28 September 1871, all children born to slaves after that date were automatically free.

which rose from the road. She could distinguish his farewell wave to her as he crossed the crest of the hill and disappeared from view.

And she did not feel sad, did not feel an emptiness around her; she even felt more comfortable being alone, in her own company, mistress of her thoughts and actions with complete freedom, even from suggestion.

Her vanity was, of course, flattered by the idea that Barbosa would think of her alone, without interruption; that her image was there alive, engraved in his memory; that she was the reference, the object, of his every thought and deed.

And, subtle analyst as she was, she did not deceive herself as to her own sentiments. In the pleasure which the subjection of Barbosa gave her she discovered more satisfaction to her flattered pride than contentment in returned love.

She went to Barbosa's room and started to put the jumble of things in order; the books and journals which cluttered the table, the marble top of the night-stand, the chairs.

No one in the house, not even the Colonel, was any longer surprised at these attentions. The close friendship, the intimacy which reigned between her and Barbosa justified them; everyone found the domestic role which she had assumed completely natural.

In the slave quarters, however, the eccentric and libertine life which she led with Barbosa was already beginning to provide matter for the characteristic malicious chatter of the negro race. The blacks, principally the women, began to murmur; commenting on the unproductive hunting, laying emphasis on certain words, spreading scandal.

Pulling open a drawer of Barbosa's table to put away the small objects which she had found scattered about, Lenita came across an oblong, tortoiseshell box, incrusted with metal and mother-of-pearl.

She opened it without thinking, without curiosity. Inside she found four folded sheets of paper, a very rusty medallion of Nossa Senhora da Aparecida,[60] some dry flowers and various little tufts of loose white wool.

This made her wonder. What on earth could it be? Barbosa was not religious, the medallion could not be his. And the tufts of wool? They had certainly come from a woven shawl, a ball wrap, in which a woman had enveloped herself, had veiled herself, in order to seek him out in his house, his room, his bed. And the dry flowers? And

---
[60] Patron Saint of Brazil.

the papers? Ah! the papers... the papers certainly contained the key to the enigma, the solution to the whole affair.

She unfolded the first and found a lock of chestnut, almost black hair, very fine and silky.

The second was a *billet-doux* of just a few lines: a beautiful hand, fine and round, a woman's. It read:

I expect you on Saturday without fail; if you do not come, I shall be cross! I cannot forget you even for a moment. Farewell.

Lenita paled and bit her lip. Trembling, her eyes flashing, she opened the third paper, a big, wide, foolscap sheet of Fiume paper. It was written in Barbosa's hand, an ugly, easily legible copperplate. Evidently it was a series of impressions committed to paper on the spot, as they had occurred, unconnected, and interrupted by reticences.

Lenita read:

The train was about to leave.

She was on the platform of the Estação da Luz,[61] *with her husband, saying Goodbye to goodness knows whom. She looked at me, I looked at her; she lowered her eyes, big green eyes; she blushed. Her left arm was linked in her husband's, with an air of boredom, of irritation; the right hung loosely down her body, strong, muscular, very white. Her ungloved hand was small and shapely, with a brilliant marquise-cut stone on the ring finger. She raised her eyes to meet mine, lowered them again and advanced her right foot, an adorable little foot, and beat it frantically, as if she was thoroughly upset. Her husband said something to her in German and she replied in the same language. They left and I followed. They took the tram coming from Santa Cecilia.......................... green eyes...................... love...................... venusta flower....................*

I saw her once more.

It was in the Grand Hotel; she was dining at the centre table. She had her back to me. She was sitting back in her chair, her body leaning to the left. Her right leg, tucked behind her left, made a nervous, fluttering movement. Her tiny foot, encased in a crimson silk stocking, curved so that her Clarks shoe hung half off, displaying the delicious, round little heel. Her left foot was placed squarely on the floor. Her dress hung down over the chair, partly covering it in folds of drapery, and beneath it could be seen the very white fringe of a petticoat. The breeze which

---
[61] Railway station in São Paulo.

entered through the tall windows stirred the golden curls on the nape of her neck. She stood up, rolling to the left, her bust curved, with a graceful movement which threw into relief the exuberance of the full breasts squeezed into the tight corset, in provocative contrast to the slenderness of her waist.

The fourth paper, yellow, disintegrating along the folds, contained a poem, also written in Barbosa's hand.
Lenita read:

M.I.

Are you pretty or ugly? I know not
According to rules of the art.
I know 'tis my pleasure to watch you,
To study each part.

The silkiness of your complexion
Owes not to red roses its hue.
The cast of your cheek to the pallor
Of sickness is due.

Unearthly the flashes that sparkle,
The icy stilettos which pierce:
Blue, like the gleam on a sword-blade,
In your eyes of dulled glass.

Your lip, never still in its trembling,
Gorged with blood, ready to burst,
Seems only to seek after pleasure
With passionate thirst.

Electric, your hands twist in spasms
As if to excite with their charge.
Your body is lithe and expectant
Like a panther at large.

Would you know what I feel when I see you?
Can my tongue find a word for my fire?
T'were a lie to declare that I love you...
I am gnawed by desire.

The scales fell from her eyes: in her suddenly illuminated spirit gaped a great void, the structure of illusion crashed to the ground.

She thought — Barbosa was married in Europe; she had known that when she met him, she could not call him to account for affections which dated back to the period of his wife, the keepsakes of her which he might have preserved.

But here it was not a question of his wife; there were three women at least — one with dark hair, who must naturally have had dark eyes to match; one described in the fragment of prose as having green eyes; one from the poetic babble with eyes of steely blue.

And who was to say they were not six or seven. The *billet-doux* could be from another, the rusty medallion from another; the dry flowers from another, the tufts of white wool from another again.

And what were those little tufts of wool, if not mementos, amorous trophies, no doubt collected in an unmade bed, the sheets still warm after a night of erotic delirium?

The man was a libertine, a third-rate Don Juan; and she, Lenita, nothing more than one of his many mistresses.

Who was to say that a present of hers, some little *épave*[62] which had belonged to her, would not go to swell this ignominious collection.

What had become of her pride, the high opinion in which she held her sex, in which she held herself!

The mistress of a libertine, the trull of an old married man who kept trophies of his conquests... How lovely! How magnificent!

She was punished, and justly punished.

She had gone out to acquire superiority over other women through knowledge; and in the tree of knowledge she had found a polluting worm.

She had wanted to fly, to soar, to reach the clouds, but the *flesh* had pinned her to earth and she had fallen, submitted. Fallen like the coarse black girl in the scrub, submitted like the placid cow in the pasture. Rebelling against the social metaphysic, she had placed herself beyond the law of society, and her conscience was punishing her, testifying how far she had fallen below the common level of that same society.

It is madness to crash headlong into the product of thousands of centuries of evolution. Society is right: its foundation is the family and the foundation of the family is marriage. Love which does not tend towards sanctification through the constitution of a family,

---

[62] French: Knick-knack, trifle.

through honourable, legal marriage, accepted and recognised, is not love but animal brutality, an agitation of the senses. No, she had not loved Barbosa; that had not been love. She had sought him out, surrendered to him as the result of a disorder in her organism, a functional imbalance, a neurosis. Like Phaedra in the fable, like the daughters of Job in the Bible, like the historical wife of Claudius, she had fallen beneath the lash of the *flesh*, and, at the prompting of a highly-educated libertine, had slipped to the lowest depths, the deepest stratum of slime. No, she did not love, had never loved Barbosa. What she had felt for him had been a gradual, progressive, vicious, morbid attraction. Her first impression when she saw him had been negative; and one should trust one's first impressions, because they are produced instinctively on the unprepared spirit. Now that she was seeing Barbosa as he really was, she could see the abyss into which she had fallen. Innocent dove, she had sought the talon of the hawk, had given herself up to his claws, and he had defiled her; not only had he stolen her virginity, he had debauched her with infamous practices to arouse her unawakened senses...

She replaced all the objects in the box in disarray, threw the box into the drawer, slammed the drawer shut, left his room and returned to her own. She entered, locked the door, threw herself on the bed and burst into tears.

Suddenly she sat up.

What was she about? she asked herself. Was she a woman to weep and wail, like any serving-girl ravished by the son of the house? No! She had fallen, but she had fallen conquered by herself, and herself alone, by her organism, her nerves. The man himself had not been a factor, was no more than a mere instrument: it had been Barbosa; it might have been the administrator, it might have been the old Colonel. So long as she had desired it, she had taken her pleasure; she was satiated...

A terrible idea crossed her mind.

Recently, perhaps for the last month, she had felt herself strangely changed, morally and physically: she had become irritable, suffered fevers of impatience. She would lose her temper over a trifle, nothing at all. She was eating badly: the mere sight of the laid table provoked nausea in her, she even vomited on occasion. Her appetite had become freakish, she had extravagant cravings. One evening she had seen a bunch of *caraguatá* by the roadside: she had felt an irrepressible urge to eat, had eaten, burning her mouth with the caustic juice of the bromeliad.

With astonishment, she saw that Barbosa, for some unaccountable reason, no longer inspired admiration in her. The speeches, the scientific dissertations to which he treated her, although correct, irritated her; she found him boorish, vulgar, pretentious, to the point of developing an aversion to him. She even thought that she could smell a peculiar, nauseous smell on his body and his clothing, a sort of mousy smell. She was repelled by his caresses; in fact, to tell the truth, they made her physically uncomfortable.

She remembered the words of Rabelais: '*Les bêtes sur leurs ventrées n'endurent jamais le mâle masculant.*'[63]

Could she be pregnant?

She ran to her desk, opened a drawer and pulled out a pocket calendar. She leafed through the months, turning the pages quickly. It was 20 August, the last day marked with a red cross was St Paul's day, 29 June. The interval was fifty-two days…

She unbuttoned her bodice, eased the strap of her slip off her shoulder, and exposed her left breast, firm and round: she bent her head to inspect it, sticking out her lower lip. The aureole, normally pink and barely perceptible, was darker, brownish, accentuated, dotted with hard papillae. There was no doubt about it, she was pregnant.

She felt, or thought she felt, something wriggling, curling up in her uterus. In the same moment a wave of indescribable affection swept over her for this creature, whatever it was, which was trying out its first movements in the ante-room of life. It was like the bursting of a storm, a flood of nerves, which invaded her, inundated her, as the waters of a burst dam invade and flood a plain.

In the vast love which filled her, Lenita recognised the feeling so ridiculously elevated to the sublime by mawkish poets, so egoistic, so human, so animal: maternity.

What was she going to do? she wondered, and found the answer without hesitation. Complete the pregnancy, give birth, raise and educate the child, see herself reborn in it, be a mother.

For two days Lenita never left her apartments, except to go to occasional meals.

---

[63] 'Beasts when they are pregnant never suffer the masculating male.' *Gargantua* Ch. 3.

At lunch on the third day, a Thursday, she told the Colonel that on Sunday she meant to go to town, from there to the city, and from the city to São Paulo; her belongings were assembled, her cases packed; she needed the cart to transport them, the trap for herself; that if she left very early she would arrive in good time, might even have to wait for the train — perhaps an hour.

'What wild goose chase is this?' the Colonel enquired. 'What are you suddenly going off to do in São Paulo, without a why or a wherefore?'

Lenita's insistence, firm against every objection, led him to suggest that she should at least wait for Barbosa's return from Ipanema to escort her; she could not, must not go alone; he, the Colonel, threatened with an attack of rheumatism which was already beginning, felt himself completely incapable of doing his duty and accompanying her.

'I will be fine going just with the boy as far as town.' Lenita returned, unmoved. She had no need for a companion on the train, and it was impossible for her not to go.

The supplications of the invalid, the Colonel's pouting insistence, were fruitless.

The cart with the baggage departed on Saturday afternoon, and early on Sunday morning Lenita, wearing a light coat and a broad-brimmed hat, kissed the old woman goodbye with tears, embraced the Colonel, who was sobbing like a child, climbed into the trap and set off.

'My girl,' the Colonel called after her, choking and wiping his eyes, 'your head is all wrong but your heart is in the right place; I'm very fond of you. In any and every emergency, remember that your grand-father and I were like brothers, and that I always looked on your father as a son. This old man is at your service in absolutely any circumstances.'

And he added to himself:

'All this physicking and botanizing and hunting was bound to end in something, and it's come to this. It would have been better if the girl had never thought to come to the *fazenda*, or if Manduca had stayed down there in Paranapanema. I'll give him a warm time.'

Chapter 18

Six days after Lenita's departure, Barbosa arrived.

He knew nothing, the Colonel had not written.

From the moment he crossed the crest of the hill he started to look ahead, expecting at any moment to see the girl's form at a window, in the yard, anywhere. He looked forward to the pleasure of seeing her trembling with delight on sighting him, and running out to meet him, pale, shaking, convulsed with emotion.

He thought of the night, and a shiver ran through him; he put the thought of that pleasure far out of his mind, so as to forget also that he had so many hours to wait.

And no one appeared at the windows. Over the brown earth of the clean-swept yard, blue and red blobs moved, scurried rapidly hither and thither; it was a group of black children running and playing, dressed in their worsted shirts. That was all.

'Better still,' said Barbosa to himself. 'I'll surprise her on the veranda, chatting with the old man.'

He descended the hill, arrived at the gate.

The black children gathered in a circle, and, threatening his plan, raised their hands and started to chant in tune, in a rhythmic, cadent melopeia:

'Here come Massah, Massah done come!'

'Shut your noise, dammit!' shouted Barbosa, putting his right index finger to his lips.

The black children, trained to obedience, fell silent.

He dismounted, took off his spurs, crossed the yard, entered the house, and crept on tiptoe to the veranda.

It was deserted.

He went to his father's room, and found the Colonel in bed, groaning with rheumatism. The old invalid was nodding in her habitual *chaise-longue*.

'How are you Father? Mother?'

He kissed the hand of one and the head of the other.

'As well as could be expected,' replied the Colonel, 'still suffering… Ay!… This damned rheumatism, won't let go… How did your journey go?'

'Very well.'

'The mill?'

'On the way. It'll be at the station tomorrow.'

'So we'll have to send the carts today to wait for it?'

'They can go tomorrow.'

'And did you get something good?'

'First rate. Some of the pieces were cast specially. They made the moulds from my drawings.'

'Very good, and what did it cost?'

'It was cheap, no more than three *contos*.'

'Ha! Have you had dinner?'

'No, I haven't.'

The Colonel sat up with an effort and pulled a little key out from under his pillow. He put it to his lips and gave a long, piercing whistle.'

'Yes, Massah!' a slave shouted from within, and shortly appeared at the door of the room.

'Young Massah is here. He has not had any dinner.'

'Yes Massah, Sir.'

He turned rapidly and disappeared.

Barbosa did not like to ask for Lenita. She must be in her room. He would go and see her there.

He excused himself from his father, saying he would not be long; that he would be back shortly and they could talk.

He came to Lenita's room and felt a fist tighten round his heart when he saw the bare tables: no bronzes, no statuettes, no *sêvres* jars, no Satzuma perfume spray.

He went to the bedchamber, pushed the door, it was locked; to the other room, empty. He turned pale and leant against the door-frame to save himself from falling. What had happened? Where had she gone?

He went back to his father's room.

'Father, where's Miss Lenita?'

'If she's carried out her intention, she's in São Paulo, staying with a relation, or with Fernandes Faria, or in some hotel. Sheer lunacy.'

'But... she's gone to São Paulo?!' Barbosa exclaimed, as if denying the evidence, as if fleeing from the brutality of the fact.

'She's gone. You know her just as well as I do: once she decides on something, it's as good as done; there's no holding her.'

Barbosa fell into a chair.

He was not pale, not livid, he was both at once: there were leaden-grey blotches on the earthy hue of his face.

His features wore something of the expression which must be visible on a bronze mask which has fallen into the furnace and is starting to melt.

He remained seated for a long while, hardly answering his father's questions.

He was called to dinner. He went, sat at the table, laid his crossed arms on it, buried his head in the crook of his left arm, and sat motionless.

He reflected.

Lenita was not there: she was not in the sitting room, she was not in the bedroom, she was not in the yard, she was not in the orchard, she was not in the *fazenda*. He would never see her again, never hear her soft voice, never kiss her red lips, never drink the freshness of her breath... Alone... Alone... He was alone.

She had provoked him, she had offered herself, she had surrendered herself, she had lent herself to all his caprices, tame, docile, submissive, only to abandon him, leaving him alone with his memories, given over to the torment of loneliness.

No, it was impossible: Lenita was there, across the table from him, she had not gone...

He raised his head, opened unfocussed eyes, and saw before him only the black serving-girl, fanning away the flies, gently and lazily waving a sprig of wild rosemary to and fro.

Barbosa let his head fall again, returned to his painful meditation, like one taking pleasure in turning the knife in the wound.

How crazy he had been!

He had had dozens of mistresses, had been — still was — married; knew to its depths the nature, the capricious, neurotic, inconstant, illogical, flawed, absurd organisation of the female of the human species. He knew woman: her uterus, her flesh, her weak mind enslaved by the flesh, dominated by the uterus. And stolidly and stupidly, like an inexperienced puppy, he had let himself become entangled in a passion for a woman!

Time was passing, the dinner had gone cold.

Barbosa rose.

'Young Massah not eating?' asked the black cook sadly, observing him from the door of the passage.

'No Rita, I don't feel like it. I'm not well.'

He left the room, went to the yard door and looked round at the environs.

All nature seemed to have died, the countryside appeared to him like a vast, disproportionate corpse.

His diaphragm seemed to exert a constant, uninterrupted, painful, upward pressure on his heart, taking his breath away, suffocating him.

He wanted to weep; weeping, he thought, would do him good, relieve him. Impossible. A dry, feverish, burning sensation inflamed his eyes.

In the immobility of the ancient forest, in the impassive calm of the yellowing slopes, there was, or so it seemed to him, something hostile: this majestic indifference irritated him, seemed to deride the anguish in which his spirit was wrung.

And everything reminded him of Lenita. In the ante-room, at the door of which he was standing, he had seen her for the first time, tortured as he was by his migraine; in the orchard, of which he could just glimpse a corner, they had held their first conversation; on the pasture, which stretched away in his mind's eye, how often they had walked together; in the forest to his front, the hunting, the birds, the *cutia*, the wild pigs, the rattlesnake… ah! the rattlesnake!! Why had Lenita not succumbed to the venom of the snake? Why had he saved her life?! If she had died then, she would be no more than a sweet nostalgia, not this voracious memory which was killing him.

Night fell.

The darkness, the silence — a cruel reproduction of the darkness and silence of past nights, nights of love which would not come again — kindled and exacerbated the pain of his suffering, the onward rolling of his solitude

He thought of suicide.

'Not yet,' he said. 'Wait a little.'

He went into his room, lay down, prepared himself a morphine injection and went to sleep.

The machinery arrived next day as expected.

Barbosa threw himself into a fever of activity.

He unpacked the mill and assembled it himself. He multiplied himself, divided his person: was carpenter, mason, sawyer, engineer.

He tried to forget: during the day he hypnotised himself with work, at night with morphine.

When the mill was ready, the milling continued.

Barbosa took over the management of the milling. The sugar from the *fazenda* became famous.

'What a clever lad!' said the Colonel. 'A regular factotum! Who would have thought that he knows more about the manufacture of sugar than I do, I who have been working with cane since I was so high? Those who study, learn. But… I don't like it. The way he's behaving now isn't natural; he didn't use to be like that. That Lenita…'

One day in the first half of October the boy brought two letters from town among the correspondence, with the envelopes addressed in a beautiful, neat, round hand, a woman's hand.

Lenita.

Barbosa recognised it at once.

One letter was addressed to him, the other to the Colonel.

Barbosa took his, opened it, and pale, very pale, his hands trembling slightly, started to read.

It ran:

São Paulo, 5*th* October 1887.

To Sr. Manuel Barbosa, Greetings.

Master,
On arriving at the fazenda you will certainly have been surprised by my sudden departure.

You will have sought an explanation, you will not have found it: neither have I. Remember the words of Spinosa: 'Our illusion of free will comes from our ignorance of the motives which govern us.' In the case of my departure, I might well believe that I acted according to my free will. Besides, I am a woman, I am capricious. Who will dispute or explain the caprices of a woman? It is infinitely better non ragionar di lor,[64] *to bite one's tongue and pass on!*

How have I spent my life been since I left the fazenda? Even I cannot tell you.

Studying? No, I have not studied; I have been knowledgeable and exceptional for so long, that I find it only fair to allow myself the luxury of being ignorant, of being a woman for a little while.

But no! No-one gains knowledge with impunity. Science is a Shirt of Nessus: once you put it on it sticks to the skin, you can never take it off. When you try to remove it, it leaves bits of the lining behind: pedantry.

---

[64] Italian — 'Not to reason about them.'

The proof of this is the fact that I am writing to you, because I cannot resist the urge to communicate my impressions to you, to talk for a moment to someone who I know will understand me.

How I miss our chats at times, our lessons, in which the light of your profound knowledge did so much to dissipate the gloom of my ignorance!

But that is in the past. We were like two wandering stars which met in a corner of space, travelled together while their orbits were in parallel, and have now separated as each follows his own destiny.

To come to the point.

São Paulo today is a huge city, with sixty thousand inhabitants at the very least.

Day by day, to north and south, to east and west, it is growing, spreading, and most important of all, it is becoming more beautiful.

The horrible hovels of the end of the last century and the beginning of this are being demolished to make way for comfortable, hygienic, modern houses. The little palaces of the transition period — in either fazenda *or cosmopolitan style — without art or taste, dull and heavy but solidly constructed, are a serious defect which will not disappear. But there are works built in the last five years by the architect Ramos de Azevedo, by the Italian Pucci and other foreigners, which are real works of art. I am delighted by the Treasury Office which is being built by Ramos de Azevedo: it is a building worthy of São Paulo in the severity and elegance of its style, in its evident robustness, from the deep foundations to the tall bell-tower. The huge building forms a compact, homogeneous block, without the slightest fault, without even a crack caused by settling. When you think what was there before... Heavens above!! To remind yourself of what it was like you have only to look at the existing Government Building, built by the same hands. The ghost of Mr Florencio de Abreu[65] can wipe its hands on the walls of the Elysian Fields — if the Elysian Fields have walls! To pull down the solid, historic, legendary old construction of the Jesuits, in order to extend on the same site that frightful eyesore! I don't know why he did not knock down the chapel as well... Mr. de Parnaíba revealed the mysteries of the crypt of the Fathers of Loyola when he pulled down a door at the same level as the chapel tower. On the left as you go in you can distinctly see six burial alcoves, six catacombs, one above*

---

[65] Governor of São Paulo for a few months before his death in 1881. The Elysian Fields, in Greek mythology the dwelling-place of ghosts, was also the name of the Government Building referred to.

the other in two orders of three each, built into the thickness of the enormous wall. Were those who lie there already dead when they were introduced? Or were they walled up alive, according to the terrible law of the secret code of the Company? It is the responsibility, indeed the duty, of the government and the diocesan bishop to have the tombs opened, since they may contain important documents relating to the history of the province.

The Chá, as you will remember, was forest when I first visited São Paulo with my father. Today it is a populous quarter, consisting of a vast grid of broad, straight streets, airy and well-lit.

There are a number of cobbled streets in the city. The famous old Largo de São Francisco is a delight to walk on.

The academy has been rebuilt.

I may be wrong but I prefer the outside as it used to be. At least it had the merit of representing the architectural taste of the religious foundation which led the colonization of Brazil. To day it does not represent anything at all; its lines are clean, but it is dull to the point of fogeyism.

As the city spreads, the quarters run together, the borders between them disappear. Luz already runs into Brás along the Rua São Caetano.

Trade has developed at an extraordinary rate, and industry is following close behind.

São Paulo contains factories of furniture, hats, calico, embroidered cloth and gloves to rival Rio, and which are providing serious competition for European goods.

In São Bento and Imperatriz Streets there is an enormous concentration of shops, department stores, banking houses and establishments of every kind.

The windows of the jewellery shops compete to display wealth and taste. Here a purveyor of Swiss clocks, delicate, elegant, shows off its excellent, unmatched 'Patek Philipe'; next door are the solid artefacts of the American clock shop, Walthams: machine-made, heavy, bulky, angular, with a profusion of unfortunate ornamentation. There, silverware from Oporto, with marvellous, airy filigree, frames the reflection in its matt, pale surface of the fulvous glow of French goldsmithery, the magical scintillations of the purest diamonds of Brazil, the coloured diamonds of the Cape, of rubies, sapphires, topazes, amethysts and rainbow-hued opals. The light plays on the worked *metals and the facets of the stones in such magnificent exuberance that it makes you think of fairy-tales, of Aladdin's cave.*

Yesterday I went into a fashion house, Mascote.

My eye was caught by some Barbedienne bronzes, displayed in a showcase inside the shop.

Some were reproductions of the ones that I have: the hoplite known as the Gladiador Borghese, *the* Venus de Milo, *the* Salona Venus; *others were new to me: the* Boy with a Basket, *by Barrias, the* Bacchante with a Bunch of Grapes, *by Clodion.*

What a delightful bronze that is; how realistic the folds of the dress! What a gentle delicacy of posture! The metal face seems to possess the softness, the blurred transparency of living skin. The eyes seem to be closing in an ecstasy of voluptuousness...

It has been ordered by Júlio Ribeiro, a grammarian who appears to be anything but: he does not take snuff, or wear Alcobaça cloth, or a pince-nez, or even a top hat. He likes porcelains, ivories, artistic bronzes, antique coins. From what I hear, he has one adorable quality, a real title of merit — he never talks, never discourses, about grammatical matters.

One of the owners of the shop came to receive me, an affable boy, Parisian in his manners, with a flower in his buttonhole and an artificial smile.

I ordered one or two things: the other partner, his brother I believe, took notes so as to send them to the house; a grave, serious young man, with loyal features, always at his desk, always writing, a perfect old-style Portuguese, hard-working, honest, punctual, plodding.

Opposite is Casa Garraux, a huge Babel: in name a bookshop but in reality a luxury bazaar, where you can find anything from a rare book to lotos-fruit paste, by way of genuine Cliquot and fire-proof strong boxes.

I went to see the permanent display there.

I had hardly entered when a group of men came in, three or four if I remember rightly.

One was a stout party with a full head of hair, well-groomed, in the autumn of maturity, or better, the springtime of old age. A thick moustache, with a vein of silver here and there, and long, capriciously shaven side-whiskers which stood out clearly against his fresh complexion. His hair was divided unpretentiously by a parting in the centre of his broad, slightly rounded forehead. He wore a wing-collar, a knotted white tie, a waistcoat buttoned up to the tie-knot, a frock-

coat with an enormous flower in the buttonhole, black cashmere socks with a narrow white silk stripe, a tall soft black hat, Clarks shoes and a pince-nez.

A handsome man — Ramalho Ortigão, as you have already guessed.

One of his companions was a tall, strongly-built boy, pale, with light chestnut, almost blond, wavy hair, a curly moustache and a red, glistening lower lip: a delightful conversationalist, whom you told me you once met in Campinas, and to whom I was introduced recently at a birthday party, Gaspar da Silva.

Ramalho fell into conversation with one of the partners of Casa Garraux. I pretended to examine a book, and listened with all my ears. I picked up, dissected, analysed his every word.

A pleasant voice, well-timbred, and with clear, very correct pronunciation. A pure Lisbon accent, foreign-sounding, very strange to Paulista ears.

Ramalho Ortigão is beyond question a man for a fight, a great writer. However I do not like him. I find him too polished, too well-worked, too self-conscious; il pose toujours.[66] *He does not write like Garrett, emptying his soul onto the page: he calculates the effect of every word, of every phrase, like a chess-player calculating the scope of movement of every piece. His writing contains constant themes and quantities, which reappear as if fated. There is always an exaggerated admiration for all that is muscular vigour, all that is manifestation of human physical strength. The goad, the big stick, are indispensable factors in his theories of social moralising. His hygiene and the concern for his body form a cult which borders on the unseemly. He never misses an opportunity to tell you how he took a bath, shaved, changed his linen. He insists and protests so much that one would think that he has a secret fear of being disbelieved. He is writing a new book: his regular readers know him and are waiting for clues. He must perforce speak of suitcases, toilet articles, disinfectants, an abundance of drawers and underpants. He uses ready-made phrases, here is one by way of example: all his standards, all his banners, all his flags, all his ensigns, are always undulating gloriously, flapping in glorious undulations.*

Ramalho Ortigão's books are excellent, there is no denying it, both in content and form. They contain good sense and correct language: they teach you to think, and they teach you Portuguese.

---

[66] French — 'He is always posing.'

What I do not think they are is a mirror, a camera obscura, *for the study of the personality of the author.*

It is my impression that you cannot get to know Ramalho Ortigão by reading Em Paris, *or* Farpas, *or his part of* Mistério da Estrada de Cintra, *nor* Caldas e Praias, *nor* Impressões de Viagem, *nor* Holanda, *nor* John Bull: *he provides a better photograph of himself in his articles on the Vieira de Castro Question*[67] *than in all of these.*

At all events, yesterday was a great day for me: I met a great man.

Now, for us: what concerns us most closely...

Here followed a few lines encrypted in a cipher which Barbosa and Lenita had contrived in the early days of their companionship.

I am three months pregnant, more or less.

I need an official *father for our child:* ora pater est is quem iustae nuptiae demostrant.[68]

If you were free we would make our natural nuptials iustae in church, and that would be that. But you are married, and the divorce law here in Brazil does not permit you to remarry. I had to find another.

'Had to find' is a manner of speaking: the other stumbled across my path, offered himself to me; all I did was to accept him, and even so placed certain conditions upon him.

He is Dr. Mendes Maia.

When I arrived here I wrote to him at court; he came at once, we held a long conference, I was frank and told him everything, and... and... and we are to be married tomorrow at five o'clock in the morning... We will travel on to the court on the Northern Railway train which leaves at six, and from the court to Europe by the first steamer.

I know that you will always remember me, as I will always remember you: punning apart, what passed between us is unforgettable.

Do not hold it against me. We were to one another what we could be, nothing more, nothing less.

If the child is a boy it will be called Manuel, if a girl, Manuela.

The letter continued.

---

[67] The Portuguese writer Ramalho Ortigão wrote a contentious pamphlet against the student unrest of 1865 in the University of Coimbra, which led him to a duel. An important provoker of the unrest was the young writer José Vieira de Castro.

[68] The father is the man indicated by legal marriage.

Livid, his features horribly twisted, Barbosa tore it across twice and threw it into a miry puddle where a few pigs were wallowing with infinite delight.

'Whore! Vile prostitute!' he exclaimed.

'Do you know what?' the Colonel asked as he came up. 'Lenita is getting married! She wrote to tell me.'

'She wrote to me, too.'

'Did she? And she kept saying she didn't want to get married... Women! That's why she left so suddenly.'

'That's right,' replied Barbosa.

He spent the whole afternoon reflecting, turning it over in his mind.

In the evening he did not give himself a morphine injection but sat up all night.

The next day early he went out and walked round the orchard, went to the forest, to the bait-ring, looked at the ruins of the hide, the maize stalks which had sprouted and died without fruiting, suppressed by the lack of light. Among the dry leaves he even saw a few vertebra and ribs from the rattlesnake.

He returned, passing by the fruit tree, from the top of which came the strident sawing of an *araponga*.

He found a *jacu* feather on the ground, muddy, discoloured by the damp.

He picked it up, contemplated it for a long time and let it fall.

He returned to the house, where he refused luncheon and ordered a bath.

He undressed, stepped into the tub, lay down and turned with pleasure in the tepid water scented with Lubin vinegar.

At length he got out, dried himself carefully, put on a pair of very soft, cool, well-ironed, scented linen drawers.

He called two negroes, ordered them to take away the bath-tub and empty it.

He went to the table, took a bottle of Hungarian wine, sweet and perfumed, Rusti-Aszu; he opened it, filled a glass, held it up to the light to examine the burnt topaz transparency of the precious liquid, smelt it, inhaled the bouquet, drank in sips like the fine *connoisseur* that he was, smacking his tongue.

He pulled open a drawer and took out a long patent leather case, which he opened. Inside was a glass syringe, a porcelain capsule, a scarifier with ten blades and a curious, fat, little black clay jar, carefully stoppered with a wooden plug. A label announced the contents in red letters on a yellow ground.

Barbosa laid all this out on the marble of the night-stand.

He took the scarifier, tested its action. Nine of the blades had been broken intentionally; one remained, sharp as a razor.

Barbosa put down the scarifier, took up the little jar, and from it dropped some dark, irregular grains, with gleaming facets, into the capsule.

It was *curare*.

From the table he took a water bottle and added about two spoonfuls of water to the capsule; with the needle of the syringe he stirred it to dissolve the terrible poison.

Once the solution had mingled, turning the dark colour of strong coffee, Barbosa filled the syringe with it.

He took up the scarifier again, armed the spring, applied it to the inner surface of his left forearm and pressed the button.

There was a muffled click.

Barbosa removed the scarifier.

A tiny line, fine as a hair, made a black mark on the white skin.

A droplet of blood appeared, welled up, round, red, brilliant, ruby-like.

Barbosa laid down the scarifier and, smiling, without changing colour, picked up the syringe and held it between the index and middle fingers of his right hand; he introduced the sharp point into the incision, placed his thumb in the ring of the plunger, grasped it firmly and pushed the piston down strongly. The excess liquid from the injection spattered out, giving the impression of a sinister arachnid on the whiteness of his skin.

Barbosa threw the rest of the contents of the capsule into the chamber pot, then placed the capsule in the patent leather case, together with the little jar, the scarifier and the syringe. On a visiting card he wrote: *Poison, handle with care* and placed the card in the case also, which he shut and put back in the drawer. He went to the washstand, dampened a towel and wiped his arm, then went back to the bed and lay down, stretched out on his back.

Two minutes passed.

Barbosa felt nothing, absolutely nothing.

He tried to look at the incision, to bring his arm up to his eyes. He could not. The paralysed member refused to obey the brain.

He tried the same with his right arm, to move his legs: impossible.

He tried to shake his head, to close and open his eyes: his head shook, his eyes closed and opened.

A few more minutes passed.

He tried again to shake his head, to close and open his eyes. Impossible. The paralysis was already nearly complete, nearly total.

He did not suffer any pain, any kind of constraint.

Down in the yard, at the foot of the mill, the blacks were threshing some beans left over from July. They were singing. The distant melody came to Barbosa deadened, in soft snatches, like the *angel voices* stop on an organ. From the ceiling hung a glass bowl with an *Epidendron fragans*: Barbosa inhaled with pleasure the heady scent from the flowers of the orchid.

In his mouth he could still taste the smooth, glowing after-taste of the full-bodied Hungarian wine.

In a corner of the ceiling, house-spiders were constructing their webs: Barbosa could clearly distinguish the skilful movements of the long, slender, jointed legs, like the fingers of a phthisic.

A fly came and alighted on his face; with a hypersensitivity which was actually painful he felt the light tickling of the insect's feet. He tried to wrinkle the skin of his face to frighten it away, but he could not.

And his perception was quite clear, his intelligence perfect.

His memory was filled, invaded by a host of mythological metamorphoses of men and women into trees and rocks.

The extravagant dream of the sickly imagination of the Hellenic poets was transmuted into a palpitating reality, was outdone in the world of fact, by the mysterious action of the American poison.

'Ah!' thought Barbosa, 'if only I could dictate to somebody my experience in these moments, describe the pleasure of this gradual death, in which life slips away, runs away like a liquid. What am I at this instant? A feeling, desiring intelligence, prisoner in a dead wrapping, captive in an inert block... The spirit, the entirety of the functions of the brain, is alive, gives orders; the body is dead, does not obey. I have one foot in existence and the other in non-existence. A few minutes more and it will all be over, without suffering, without pain... Already I glimpse the Buddhist nirvana, the repose of nothingness...

'Manduca! Manduca!'

It was his father's voice calling.

A sadness stole over Barbosa; he would have liked to reply, but he could not.

'Teresa!'

'Massah?'

'Where is Manduca? Have you seen him?'

'Yes, Massah. He in his room. He was taking a bath. Pedro and José brought the tub out just now.'

'Why the devil doesn't he answer? Unless he's asleep...'

The Colonel came to the room and entered.

When he found his son naked from the waist up, stretched out on his back on the bed, pale, motionless, his eyes open in a fixed stare, the Colonel stopped short.

'Manduca! What the... Manduca?!'

Seizing his son, clasping him round, he shook him nervously.

Barbosa's body, warm, flaccid, yielded to his father's efforts like a corpse before *rigor* sets in.

His brain, active, lucid, in full exercise of its functions, lived, understood, felt, had a will, longed to speak, to answer his father; but it no longer had organs, it was isolated from the world.

'He's dead! My son! He's dead!' roared the Colonel and rushed out distraught, his head in his hands.

This shout produced a sort of miracle.

The old invalid tensed her hands on the arms of the *chaise-longue*, and with a superhuman effort raised herself, then fell to her knees and began to crawl towards her son's room, with movements of her almost destroyed joints which would have been ridiculous, had they not been horrific.

Half naked, indecent in her nightdress, jerking and swaying like a mutilated insect as she crawled across the floor, she reached her son, reached the bed, pulled herself up; grasping the mattress, moving with agonising difficulty, she embraced the body in her turn, placed her soft, cold, wrinkled old lips against his.

At his mother's kisses, kisses which he could not return, Barbosa felt overwhelmed by a strange feeling, a filial tenderness which he had never known.

Mother! Father!

Why had he not devoted himself, with all his powerful faculties, to lessening the suffering of this old couple, to softening the miseries of their old age?!

Disillusioned with friends, lovers, wife; atheist, world-weary, sick even of himself, he had gone to seek, in frosty, exclusivist science, the death, the extinction of the last remains of affection.

He had become selfish, had become cruel.

And he still had ties to this world; he had a father, a mother to devote himself to, had someone to live for!

What a cruel revenge nature exacts!

It had handed him over, bound hand and foot, to the caprices of a hysterical woman who had offered herself to him, surrendered to him, as she would have offered herself, surrendered to any other man, a negro, a plantation slave, not for physical love but to satisfy the hungering flesh...

Replete, satiated, she had abandoned him.

In the almost cold ashes of his mortal beliefs had flared up for a moment the light of love, had shone the fire of faith, only to be extinguished at once; and the darkness had returned, thicker than ever.

Lenita had gone to seek, had found, a vile man who would sell her his name to cover her error, who would accept her as his wife, dishonoured, pregnant...

Pregnant... she was pregnant, he was going to be a father...

And she had fled from him, taken away his child; and still she was gulling him, describing to him in a cynical missive her traveller's observations, her artist's impressions! Worse still, she advised him, consciously and in advance, of her marriage to the minotaur; informed him that his, Barbosa's child was to give the august name of *father* to a man of no dignity, a cheap peddler in honour.

And he was dying for love of this woman, dying because she had broken his strength of mind, dying because she had caught him in the toils of the *flesh*, dying because life without her had become impossible... Coward!

Remorse, personified in the pitiful, all but fetid figure of his unfortunate mother, lay upon him, embracing him, devouring him, drinking his last breaths.

Oh! He wanted to live!

And it was not impossible.

If there had been someone there who understood physiology, who could establish artificial respiration until the poison was completely eliminated, death would be held at bay, life would return.

If circumstances were different, if the patient were another, Barbosa would save him.

But for himself he could do nothing: imprisoned in his body, like a butterfly in its chrysalis, he was impotent, he was powerless: he was not even granted the sorry consolation of asking, begging his poor mother for her forgiveness, this miserable invalid who had been cured in an instant by her anguish.

The placidity of a painless death, death by paralysis of the motor nerves, was changed into a frightful, ghastly torment, beyond the powers of human description!

Alive in death!

Everything was dead; only the brain lived on, only the consciousness lived, and lived in torment…

Why had he not blown out his brains with a bullet?

The paralysis invaded the last redoubts of his organism, his heart, his lungs; systole and diastole ceased; the fabrication of haematose was interrupted. As it were a veil smothered, darkened Barbosa's intelligence, and he plunged into that deep sleep from which there is no awakening.

MHRA New Translations

The guiding principle of this series is to publish new translations into English of important works that have been hitherto imperfectly translated or that are entirely untranslated. The work to be translated or re-translated should be aesthetically or intellectually important. The proposal should cover such issues as copyright and, where relevant, an account of the faults of the previous translation/s; it should be accompanied by independent statements from two experts in the field attesting to the significance of the original work (in cases where this is not obvious) and to the desirability of a new or renewed translation.

Translations should be accompanied by a fairly substantial introduction and other, briefer, apparatus: a note on the translation; a select bibliography; a chronology of the author's life and works; and notes to the text.

Titles will be selected by members of the Editorial Board and edited by leading academics.

Alison Finch
General Editor

Editorial Board

Professor Malcolm Cook (French)
Professor Alison Finch (French)
Professor Ritchie Robertson (Germanic)
Dr Mark Davie (Italian)
Dr Stephen Parkinson (Portuguese)
Professor David Gillespie (Slavonic)
Professor Derek Flitter (Spanish)
Dr Jonathan Thacker (Spanish)

Published titles

1. *Memoirs of Mademoiselle de Montpensier (La Grande Mademoiselle)* (P. J. Yarrow. Edited by William Brooks. 2010)

2. Júlio Ribeiro, *Flesh* (Translated by William Barne. 2011)

For details of how to order please visit our website at:
www.translations.mhra.org.uk

Lightning Source UK Ltd.
Milton Keynes UK
178206UK00001B/7/P